Death in West Wheeling

Death in West Wheeling

by

Homer Deters

(Not to be confused with that

Greek feller who wrote war

and adventure stories)

as told to

MICHAEL DYMMOCH

Five Star • Waterville, Maine

This novel is a work of fiction. Names, characters, places and incidents are either the product of the author's imagination, or, if real, used fictitiously.

First Edition
First Printing: September 2006

Published in 2006 in conjunction with Tekno Books and Ed Gorman.

Set in 11 pt. Plantin by Christina S. Huff.

Printed in the United States on permanent paper.

Library of Congress Cataloging-in-Publication Data

Dymmoch, Michael Allen.
Death in West Wheeling / by Homer Deters (Not to be confused with that Greek feller who wrote war and adventure stories) as told to Michael Dymmoch.—1st ed.
p. cm.
ISBN 1-59414-458-3 (hc : alk. paper)
1. Sheriffs—Fiction. 2. Illinois—Fiction. I. Title.
PS3554.Y6D425 2006
813′.54—dc22 2006005601

For
Clifford D. Grandt

Acknowledgements

This is a work of fiction. All of the characters depicted are products of the author's imagination. If they resemble real persons, it is because humans are more alike than different; realistic characterization reflects this. Homer Deters is not related (except, perhaps, in spirit) to Gary Deters, Associate Professor of Law Enforcement at Oakton Community College, to whom the author is grateful for much technical assistance. Also in order are thanks to Richard A. Schaefer (from whom I stole some great lines) for advice on rural life and expressions; to Joe Falasco and the gang at Falasco's Automotive; to James O'Shea, Law Enforcement Chair, Oakton Community College; Instructor Dennis A. Ramsey, and James G. Schaefer. I've taken liberties with the information given me. Any errors are my own.

Thanks also to the reference librarians at the Northbrook Public Library, Northbrook, Illinois; Judy Duhl and her staff at Scotland Yard Books, Winnetka, Illinois; Janis Irvine and her staff at The Book Bin, Northbrook, Illinois; Teresita, Soon Ja, and Chong at the U.S. Post Office, Northbrook, Illinois; and the Red Herrings of Scotland Yard Books. All of you helped me bring West Wheeling to life.

MAD

"I swear to tell the truth, the whole truth, an' nothin' but the truth, so help me, God. For the record, my name is Ajax Deters—though I mostly go by Homer—and I'm sheriff of Boone County. An' if you want I should tell you how I come to arrest the defendant *for murder, I reckon I oughtta start at the get-go . . ."*

how it all begun

The back of Grandpa Ross's house faces down a south slope that's been cleared of pines an' brush. So it only has big ol' trees with branches low enough to make shade, an' high enough so they ain't in the line of fire. Grandpa gener'ly sits in the kitchen, leanin' over his elbows an' breathin' like a horse with heaves. He's got what the docs called emphysema, an' his whole body sways forward an' back. An' he's thin as a rail fence—so thin his pants won't stay up without suspenders, an' he can't weigh more'n 130 pounds for all he was six feet tall once. Grandpa's got sparse white hair an' a dirty gray beard that he combs through, from time to time, with his fingers, which're yellow from smokin'. He allus sits under a light that makes his face look like death warmed over, with his hands hangin' down 'tween his knees, an' a cigarette hangin' from his fingers by sheer habit. Keeps his coffee, or shine or whatever he's havin', in a old Stagecoach Cafe mug on the floor 'tween his feet.

The way the kitchen's laid out, Grandpa kin sit with his back to the windows an' watch the yard in the big mirror over the sink. At the time the trouble started, he must've been sixty or so, but with the hard years he had on him, he looked closer to eighty. Folks all think he's wiser than anyone. Maybe he is—he's mostly got the sense to keep his mouth shut, so nobody knows for sure.

Anyway, the day it all started, he was parked in his usual spot. Rye Willis (no relation to Bruce, though he *is* related to damn near every livin' soul in Boone County) had stopped by with a sample of his latest batch of shine in a mayonnaise jar, to get the old man's opinion an' fill him in on all the local news. With both of 'em smokin', you could'a cut the air with a knife. Nina was there, too. It was late afternoon Saturday, so she was off from the post office. She was prob'ly the real reason Rye showed up. Seemed like he was rackin' his brain for any recent event he could think to tell the old man, anythin' to stretch his stay. Everyone knew he needed a wife an' he was sweet on Nina. Fat chance he had with her, even if he wasn't fifteen years older. Nina's the smartest of the old man's get, too smart to settle for the likes of Rye, too smart to smoke even. She was near twenty that summer, for all she'd been runnin' the post office goin' on three years. She was samplin' Rye's brew, too, out of one of those little half-size Mason jars. I was the only one holdin' back 'cause I was on duty. (My boss didn't cotton to havin' his deputies roll up smellin' like a still.)

Anyway, it 'peared Nina was startin' to get bored with Rye's *i*dea of current events when he threw out his ace. "That lay-brother-religious-fellow finally threw in the towel." Rye sounded surprised.

"Left town?" I said.

"Ash Jackson run him out," Nina *o*pined. "Been fillin' the heads of all the young 'uns with ideas of education." Not that Nina was opposed to schoolin'.

"Why'd Ash give a damn?" Rye demanded.

"One of 'em's Angie Boone," Nina said. "Ash's sweet on her."

"But she's his cousin," Rye said. "An' she can't be but fifteen or so."

"Lotta that runnin' round in Ash's family," Nina told him.

Rye shook his head an' changed the subject. "When're you gonna give in an' go out with me, Nina?"

"How 'bout January 26, 2102?"

I grinned. I could tell by the look she shot me that she appreciated there wasn't two dim bulbs lightin' up her life just then. The old man got it, too, almost killed hisself laughin' 'cause it started him on a coughin' fit.

"When're you gonna go out with Homer?" Rye axed her when Grandpa'd got his breath back. Rye meant me, Ajax "Homer" Deters (though nobody's called me "Ajax" since I broke Ash Jackson's jaw for makin' fun of me in the second grade).

Anyway, Nina give me a sizin'-up look, then said, "When he gets done his schoolin'." I could feel myself go red down to the soles of my feet. Nina added, "You'll have to ask *him* when that's gonna be."

I was saved from further *em*barrassment by the ruckus that broke out next. Nina's cat come streakin' through the room an' knocked over the jar of shine, causin' Grandpa to sit up an' grab behind him for his twenty-gauge. Rye swung a kick at the cat that would've killed it if he'd connected. He hates cats anyway, an' the waste of all that good liquor gave him a excuse to go after this one. Fortunately for the cat, Rye don't move a lot faster than he thinks; the critter 'scaped back the way it come. Nina grabbed the twenty-gauge from Grandpa an' would've perforated Rye with it, but I took it away from her an' removed the shells.

Grandpa wheezed, "Homer, you gimme my gun."

So I stuck it back in the corner an' tole him I'd run him in if he didn't stay out of it.

Nina ducked out the back door an' took off runnin'. Rye hit the doorjamb on his way out after her, an' that slowed him enough to let him see he hadn't a prayer of catchin' up. He stopped just outside the door, an' the two of us watched her disappear round the side of the house. She was pretty as a half-growed doe, but I personally would'a rather messed with a momma bear.

postal regulations

Nina was in the middle of settlin' a labor dispute the next Monday when I come into the post office, just after nine in the mornin'. She an' Len Hartman—he's one of West Wheeling's two mail carriers—was faced off across the counter.

Nina was sayin', "You're lucky it's just two streets an' they're short an' close together. It could be two *long* streets on the opposite ends of town."

"Where's it say in the rules I gotta take on more work 'cause Ed's gettin' too old to cut it anymore?" Len meant Ed Smithson, West Wheeling's other mailman.

"I'll show you where." Nina reached for somethin' under the counter an' I thought she was goin' for the twelve-gauge she keeps there to *dis*courage payroll robberies. Len must'a thought so too, 'cause he turned white an' took a step back. But Nina just come up with her ratty old copy of the Gideon's Bible. She slapped it on the counter with a crack like a .22 shot, an' flipped it open an' paged through it. "There!" she said, pointing. " *'Of everyone to whom much has been given, much will be required.'* "

Len scowled. "Don't it also say somethin' about the laborer bein' worthy of his hire?"

"Luke, chapter ten, verse seven," Nina said. "I could also quote Matthew twenty, one through sixteen. What's yer point?"

"I ain't gonna do it!"

"Fine! Then I ain't gonna sign your paycheck. What d'you think of that?"

Len got real red an' walked out before he could say what he thought.

Nina seemed to forget him soon as he was outta sight. "What kin I do for you, Homer?"

I was lookin' at the stack of wanted posters Nina had push-pinned to the wall next to the counter. There ain't room to post 'em all individual, so she rotates the stack from time to time. The current featured felon was Henry Highmoor. Nina'd highlighted his face, name, an' description, *child molester,* with yellow, an' penciled in: "This guy is armed an' dangerous. Shoot first. Call Homer later. An' for God's sake don't miss!"

"You sent for *me,"* I said.

"Oh. Yeah. There was a guy from the city here earlier askin' about that religious fella that Ash Jackson run off."

"That's the second time you've made that allegation. Did you *see* Ash run that fella off, or are you just spreadin' malicious rumors?"

"It's logic, is all."

"Well bein' as I'm a representative of the law, I need somethin' more'n logic. Some kind of evidence would be nice."

Nina shrugged.

"What about this city fella?"

"He was here askin' for the religious fella's forwardin' address. I told him I couldn't give it to him without a court order. He went away, but I figure he'll be back once he's been out to the mission an' don't get nothin' more outta them."

"How d'you know he needs a court order to get someone's forwardin' address?"

"Regulations."

I pointed to the Bible. "You gonna quote more outta that?"

"Nope." Nina put the Bible back under the counter an' reached a big, dark blue book off the desk behind her. "I'm gonna quote you outta this." It was the U.S. Postal Regulations.

I didn't doubt she had that memorized, too. Workin' in the post office, she's got a lot of time to read. I said, "I'll take your word for it. What if a peace officer should want to know about this religious fella's forwardin' address?"

"A peace officer'd need a court order, too. But I can tell *you*. He didn't leave no forwardin' address."

"What you been doin' with his mail?"

"Nothin.' It's all here. If he shows up or sends me a forwardin' address, I'll see he gets it."

"Why couldn't you just tell the city fella that?"

"What business is it of his? Which reminds me. You might want to be here to back me on this'n. Him bein' from the city, he might not take it well if I have to draw down on him to get him to listen to reason."

I guessed not. Particularly as there seemed to be a permanent open season in post offices. "You want I should tell him not to worry, seein' as you postal employees only shoot each other?"

"Ain't you the comedian today? You gonna help me out?"

How could I refuse Nina anything? But why'd I be fool enough to tell her so? I said, "I s'pose. Why'n't you give me a ring if he comes back?"

"Oh, he'll be back. Thanks, Homer."

I nodded. As I was leaving, I spotted Nina's hand-lettered sign on the porch: ALL SNAKES ON THIS PREMISES ARE THE PROPERTY OF THE WEST WHEELING POST OFFICE—DON'T MESS WITH 'EM. It was a pretty safe bet that city fella wouldn't understand.

how I met Nina

First time I laid eyes on Nina was the winter I got outta the service. She was jailbait then—not more'n fifteen. She was washin' school busses for the now *de*funct United Transit Corp. I come in lookin' for work an' get invited to have coffee an' donuts in the shop with my ol' grammar school buddy, Dwayne Truck. Dwayne was shop foreman at the time. Anyway, we's standin' round the coffeemaker, shootin' the breeze, when somebody notices a suspicious bunch of men collectin' out on the road near the driveway. When two of 'em breaks off from the group an' heads for the office, Dwayne calls up front to see what's brewin'. He comes back lookin' like a storm fixin' to break out, an' says, "Sheriff's come to take the stock. Seems like somebody had a lien on 'em an' got a court paper to take 'em away."

Just then, Nina comes in, an' I spot her without really noticin'. She's got her hair up in twin pony tails an' she's wearin' hip boots, an' a short raincoat, an' tight jeans. She looks about twelve years old, so it seems kinda funny her helpin' herself to coffee'n standin' there with the guys to drink it. An' nobody but me takes any notice.

Dwayne says, "Boss's on the phone to his lawyer, try'na git a court order to stop 'em, but *he'll* have to go to court an' that'll take hours. By that time, the sheriff an' his posse'll be outta state with them busses."

Just then, Nina pipes up. "D.W., what'd happen if a bus just happened to stall in the driveway in front of the office? I mean, the owner of that car that's parked there's gone for the day, ain't he?"

We all look out. Richard Truck's old, rusty white Caddy is sittin' T-crossed to the driveway, stickin' out in the in-bound lane because of the half-assed plow job the snow crew'd done.

Richard, Dwayne's younger brother, is standin' right next to Dwayne. "I shore am," he says. "May not be back 'til tomorrow sometime."

Dwayne thinks about it for all'a thirty seconds, then says, "I dunno. Lemme ask the boss." He gets on the phone for a while, then comes back an' tells Nina, "Go fer it."

We-all watch as she opens the front garage door an' starts up the bus she just washed. It's a pusher, one of them flat-fronted things with the engine in back. She weaves it down the driveway, towards the street, like she don't quite know which way she's goin' with it, then—just about even with the office—she gets in the right lane an' cuts left, 'cross both lanes of the drive. When she's just past Richard's old Caddy, she starts backin' up, jerkin', like she's got it in the wrong gear. Then she stalls it. The bus's a old diesel; Nina must'a hit the emergency cut-off switch, which disconnects the fuel line, 'cause she spends the next five minutes crankin' the starter an' wearin' the battery down without turnin' it over.

'Bout the time she gives up an' gets outta the bus, the boss comes outta the office, trailin' the sheriff. We hear him ask, "What happened?" all the way in the shop. From where we're watchin', we can see her give a little shrug, like she's embarrassed. The boss says, "Get in there an' tell Dwayne to fix it." He sounds mad, but nobody could'a planted a roadblock better than that bus was parked.

Nina walks back to the shop head down an' scuffin' her

boots on the blacktop like she's goin' to a funeral. As she comes through the doorway, though, I notice her shoulders shakin', an' she barely gets inside 'fore she busts out laughin'.

"*You're* on, D.W.," she says.

Dwayne gets a handful of wrenches from his tool box an' goes out to make sure nobody can move that sucker 'til the boss gives the word. It ain't long 'fore he has engine parts laid out all over the drive. The boss comes out an' does some armchair quarterbackin' for the sheriff's benefit—that we can hear all the way in the shop. Pretty soon, Dwayne starts throwin' his tools down like this tail-bitin' is the last straw. "If you don't like the way I'm doin' it," he tells the boss, "fix the damn thing yourself!" Then he turns round an' stalks back to the shop, where we-all give him a round of applause.

"Dwayne, what's to keep the sheriff from callin' someone to come fix it?" Patrick Truck says.

"Nothin'," says Dwayne. "But he'll have a hell of a time fixin' it without these." He holds up a handful of small parts he'd took out. "Don't guess Call an' Haul carries spare bus parts in their rig."

"Hey, Dwayne," someone says. "Here comes the boss."

Boss comes in without the sheriff. He hands Dwayne a fifty-dollar bill an' says, "You-all go to lunch. An' if anybody asks, I'm a son-of-a-bitch an' you're lettin' your union rep work all this out."

Dwayne says, "Sure thing. But how're we supposed to get out with that bus blockin' the drive?"

The boss was halfway out the door by then. He says, "Call an effin' cab for all I care. Just get lost for a couple hours."

Which is what we done. We all piled into my van, 'cause it was the only vehicle that wasn't trapped by the bus, an' went to KFC. By the time we got back, the sheriff an' his posse was gone. Dwayne fixed the bus, an' Nina backed it up—all the way round the shop building.

While we was watchin' her park, Dwayne said, "Homer, you got any sense a-tall, you'll marry that gal. I'd do it myself, but I already got a good woman."

"Be kinda robbin' the cradle, wouldn't it, Dwayne? What is she, fifteen?"

"I ain't sayin' this week, man. But she's definitely worth the wait."

John Peter

When the city fella come back, I was sittin' on the front porch of the post office with my feet up on the railin', doin' my best Deputy Redneck imitation. I could see right off why Nina'd made him for a stranger. Only lawyers, insurance salesmen, an' undertakers wear suits in town on weekdays. 'Fore he noticed me, he stopped to stare at Nina's sign. She posted it after she caught a couple of local geniuses tryin'a set fire to a nest of baby garter snakes. Nina's no more partial to snakes than the next person, but she's smart enough to know snakes eat rats an' mice an' usually don't bother people unless they're messed with.

The man give his head a little shake—like he was tryin'a wake hisself up—then looked at me. He pointed at the sign an' said, "What's that about?"

I told him the story. By the time I'd done, I could see him lookin' for snakes outta the corners of his eyes.

"You mean they keep snakes to control vermin?"

I shrugged. "Cheaper'n Decon, an' you don't have to clean up dead critters."

"That's crazy!"

"You didn't come all this way to criticize our extermination methods."

He pulled hisself together an' said, "I'm a private detective. I—"

"No foolin'? You got a license an' everythin'?"

"I have a license . . ."

He went to reach somethin' outta his inside pocket, an' I said, "Hold it!" He froze. "You got a gun in there?"

He gave a little sigh an' said, "No, just a wallet."

I give him a nod an' he pulled it out an' took out his license. *John Peter,* I read off it. "What brings you to West Wheeling, Mr. Peter?"

"I'm looking for Roger Devon." The way he said it rhymed with heaven.

"The missionary fella?"

"Yes. He's been missing a month. His parents are frantic. They've hired me to find him."

"How old'd this Devon be?"

"Twenty-six."

"Last time I looked ain't no law says a twenty-six-year-old fella has to account for his whereabouts to his folks."

"He's a devoted son. And it's quite out of character for him to let a whole month go by without contacting them, at least to let them know he'll be away."

"Ah-hunh. How come nobody's filed a missin' person report on this guy? Or checked the local hospital or jail?" I didn't add, *Or the coroner,* but it occurred to me.

"That's what I'm here to do. I thought I would check to see if he's having his mail forwarded, but I ran into a little opposition from your . . ."

"Postmistress?"

"Ah, yes."

"Yeah. Well, if you want that information, you're gonna have to go to court an' convince a judge he's really missin' an' you're workin' for who you said."

"Oh, please. Who else would I be working for?"

I shrugged. "He might be a protected witness, an' you

might be workin' for the mob."

"I think you've been watching too much TV, Sheriff."

I didn't dignify that crack with a answer.

Peter said, "How do I go about filing a missing person report?"

"Consider it filed."

"And where do I go to get a court order?"

I pointed out the town hall an' axed him where'd he be stayin'.

"Have you a Motel Six around here?"

" 'Bout halfway back to the highway."

"I'll stay there." He started to walk away.

"One more thing, Mr. Peter." He stopped. "Any snakes you might encounter anywhere in Boone County other'n the post office premises are the property of the department of conservation. Leave *them* be, too."

He just walked away, shakin' his head. I went inside to tell Nina she'd had a reprieve.

Father Ernie

West Wheeling's a pretty civilized place. All the major thrufares bypass downtown, so you can cross a street without fear for your life. We don't have a park district, but we got a nice little village green with shade trees an' park benches an' a Civil War statue for the pigeons. Facin' the park is the post office, where I prefer to hang out. Across the street is the town hall, which houses the mayor's office an' my office, an' the local branch office of the County Aid. The public library is in the town hall basement. We got nearly a thousand books. The Congregational Church uses the council room for Sunday service, an' the grammar school uses it for school plays.

I mostly don't pry into folks' business 'less they make trouble, or they ax me to, or unless they do somethin' odd enough to rouse my curiosity. The missionaries never made trouble or axed me for nothin', an' nothin' in the religion business in Boone County was out-of-the-ordinary enough to be called odd. But a missin' person is somethin' we don't get every day. Just the allegation was enough excuse for me to go out an' ax questions at the mission.

The town ain't real big, but we got a Saveway an' a Shell station. Also a generic drug store/dry goods, a bank, a feed store, a restaurant, a doctor, a dentist, two lawyers, a undertaker, a grammar school, three churches, an' four bars. Three of West Wheeling's bars got satellite TV, so you can place a friendly bet on any sports team on the planet. We're not big enough to have a high school, so the kids get bussed to County High. Halfway to Okra, the next closest town, we got a Wal-Mart an' a Best Buy. The nearest hospital is only twenty minutes away. In order to conduct a proper missin' person investigation, I'd have to canvass every one of them places, but first I thought I'd better head out to the Pine Ridge Mission an' talk to the missionaries, maybe get a photo so I knew what the fella I was lookin' for looked like. It'd be the first time I'd been there in the two years since they opened.

Lotta times, you can learn most about somebody from his competition, which is why I decided to drop in on Father Ernie 'fore I headed out. Ernie's the pastor of our local Catholic church, but he's a Vietnam veteran an' he was married for a time so he ain't a ordinary priest. He's probably got more horse sense than book learnin', which is sayin' a lot because he's got a Ph.D. in somethin' or other. Ernie won't tell people's secrets—somethin' to do with "the sanctity of the confessional"—but he's more'n willin' to share his observations about 'em with his friends. His take on Roger Devon was "a little green. Young and probably overoptimistic, but profoundly decent." Devon could'a took that reference to the bank.

Father Ernie never talks about his former life—it almost seems like the bishop cut him full-growed off a priest bush. No one'd ever accuse him of bein' naive. He's near as cynical as most cops, but my ma calls him a closet romantic. Rumor has it he joined the Church on the rebound—after a romantic disaster.

"Anythin' else?" I axed him.

"For instance?"

"Like any signs of insanity or unstability?"

"Not that I've seen or heard."

"When was the last time you seen him?"

"Over a month ago, maybe six weeks. It was my understanding that he resigned and went home."

"His family's filed a missin' person."

"I see."

"What can you tell me about the mission an' their reverend head honcho?"

"You know what they do out there?"

"Yeah, but gimme your version."

"You planning to sign up?" I give him a look, an' he shrugged. "They run a boarding school for disadvantaged boys and day classes for girls, ditto. The best thing they do is give kids with no hope for a future enough education to get a toe-hold in the modern world. At worst, their brand of fundamentalist Christianity is out of touch with the present century."

I nodded. "What about the reverend?" I meant the Reverend Alfred Moody, the mission CEO.

"He's good-hearted and sincere, and I'm sure he believes every word he utters. I'm just *not* sure he ever thinks about what he's saying."

the Pine Ridge Mission

The Reverend Alfred Moody reminds me of baby mice—pink an' nearly hairless, with puffy slits for eyes an' a little sucky mouth. An' his hair an' whiskers're so white an' fine they look almost see-through.

The head missionary was just about as useful, an' not a whole lot more helpful than Rye Willis's rumors. He pretty much repeated what Peter'd told me. Moody weren't worried so much as annoyed by the defection of one of his staff. He sounded like a man who wasn't unsure of his facts very often. An' he was puzzled.

"It's not that he just disappeared," the Reverend tole me. "He left a letter of resignation. What's strange is that he didn't resign in person. He didn't say anything to anyone—just folded his tent, so to speak, and vanished overnight. Very inconsiderate, I must say."

"He take his things?"

"Most of them. That's odd, too. He took his clothes and car, but left his books—even the Bible his parents gave him. And he didn't mention them in his letter of resignation. I don't know if he meant us to keep them or if he plans to send for them."

I axed him what kind of car Devon drove—an old gray Escort—an' the name an' address of his next of kin—Mr. an' Mrs. Ansel Devon of Illinois. He didn't know nothin' about

Devon's friends or extracurricular activities.

"He got along well with the children. In fact, some of them are quite upset about his leaving."

"Which ones?"

"Well . . . You'll have to ask *them*—you won't frighten them?"

"Why'd I wanna do that?"

"Well . . . er . . . Some of them have been brought up to fear representatives of the law . . ."

"Gotcha. How 'bout if I leave my gun an' badge in the car an' jus' tell 'em I'm a friend of Roger's?"

"That would be acceptable. As long as you don't lie."

I shrugged. It takes all kinds.

"The children will be breaking for lunch soon. I'll ask the teachers to cooperate fully with your . . . uh . . . investigation."

" 'Preciate that, Reverend. Jus' one more thing?"

"What is it?" He set down in the chair behind his desk, an' I could see he was dyin' to wipe the sweat off his face, only he didn't want me to notice he *could* sweat.

"D'you have a pi'ture of Devon? It'd be a damn—er, pardon—a heck of a lot easier to find him if I knew what he looked like."

I left my sidearm an' badge in my squad car, locked in the glove box, an' the pi'ture—Devon holdin' a guitar, between a kid with a fiddle an' one with a banjo—on the passenger seat. For good measure, 'cause there prob'ly ain't fifteen people over the age of ten in Boone County who can't slim-jimmy a car open in twenty seconds flat, I put my stuffed rattlesnake, Clyde, on the seat on top of Devon's pi'ture, where anybody thinkin' to trespass'd see him an' have second thoughts. Clyde looks pretty convincin' if you throw somethin' over the dog-bite holes in his middle, which I did. On the way back to the schoolyard, I cut a couple a switches off the Reverend's willow tree. In the yard, I found me a seat in the shade an' proceeded to cut the switches into sticks the right size for whistles. Pretty soon, I had the first whistle done an' was testin' it. The kids started swarmin' around like I was the Pied Piper, elbowin' each other out of the way, an' pesterin' to know who I was an' how to "make them worthless sticks sing." I told them I was a friend of Mr. Devon an' I'd be obliged if anyone could tell me where to find him. Nobody could, but I hung around 'til all the kids had more or less got the hang of makin' whistles.

Sheriff Rooney

I figured my next stop—'fore I headed out to Best Buy—ought to be the sheriff's house, to fill him in on the investigation. Sheriff Rooney's been pretty much housebound the last two years, after his stroke. That didn't stop folks reelectin' him last year. Mrs. Rooney—Martha—an' I campaigned for him with the slogan IF IT AIN'T BROKE, DON'T FIX IT. It probably helped that there's almost no crime in the county, an' the sheriff's main competitors were Rufus "Ruthless" Groggins, head of our local KKK chapter, an' Diamond Jim "I'll cover all bets" Bradley. They split the block of voters likely to elect a crook between 'em, so Sheriff Rooney won by a West Wheeling landslide—twenty votes. Both Ruthless an' DJ called for a recount, but the town council, which is also the county board, don't like to waste their time or money on lost causes.

Martha let me in the kitchen door with a cheerful, "Good to see you, Homer. You're just in time for lunch."

I hung my hat on the peg by the door an' said, "Mornin', Sheriff," to Ben, who was sittin' in his wheelchair by the table.

The sheriff didn't say nothin' back. Since the stroke, he can't move his right side or talk worth a damn, but he's developed into a world-class listener. I filled him in on recent events an' gossip while Martha put a couple more pork chops in the skillet an' peeled a few extra taters. In no time, she'd laid out a spread made me feel I'd died an' went to heaven. Ever since my ma moved to Florida for her arthritis, Martha's got my vote for best cook in the state. Odd thing is, she's also a dead shot with any kind of weapon. Ben an' Martha's been married nearly forty years. They had three sons. The oldest was killed in 'Nam. The other two grew up, married, an' moved away. They don't come to visit much.

Ben can feed hisself pretty well if Martha cuts the food up for him. She did, an' we set to packin' it away. After we finished, I helped Martha clear the plates. While she made another pot of coffee, I took out the pi'ture the Reverend Moody'd give me an' tole Ben, "I plan to run this by Merlin Willis, over at Best Buy, see if he can't blow it up into one of those 'Have you seen this man?' posters."

Ben grunted like he thought that was a good idea. Martha just smiled. When I finished my coffee an' took my leave, the Rooneys were just sittin' down to watch Marty Stouffer on their satellite TV.

Merlin Willis

Rye Willis's youngest brother got his job at Best Buy 'cause of his name. Folks figured with a name like Merlin, he had to be some kind of wizard. As a matter of fact, all the Willises are pretty talented, one way or another, from Rye, who can make a magical brew outta damn near anythin' edible, to San Antonio Willis, who can fiddle the birds outta the trees. Merlin's a wizard with anythin' *e*lectronic. He hadn't been workin' at BB six months when he had computers down cold. You'd never know it to look at him, either. He looks like the captain of the high school football team or some state police rookie. He's also a cracker-jack salesman 'causecause he tries to find out what you need somethin' for 'fore he tries to sell it to you.

"Merlin," I said, as I handed him the pi'ture Reverend Moody'd give me. "What can you do with this?"

He looked it over. "I could scan it into the computer and give each of these good ol' boys a surfboard; or put Vanna White in the lineup; or dress 'em all in Federation uniforms and move 'em to the bridge of the Enterprise." He handed me back the pi'ture.

"What I had in mind was more like a re-run of this pi'ture, an' a dozen or so eight-by-ten head shots of the *gui*tar player."

Merlin pretended to sniff. "Waste of my talent. The drugstore in West Wheeling could do that for you."

"I need 'em today. I'm willin' to pay ten bucks."

Merlin held out his hand. I give him back the pi'ture an' a ten-dollar bill from my wallet. Then I played video games on one of his demo machines while he did what he does to fill my order. He uses a computer an' color printer instead of a photo-processin' rig. He printed out a eight-by-ten of the whole pi'ture, then played with it on his computer screen 'til he had a blow-up of just Devon. Without bein' axed, he put a frame around the face an' *Wanted* under it. "What's he wanted for, Homer?"

"Maybe you'd better make that *missin',*" I said. It weren't a bad idea. I gave him the particulars—missin' since, an' whatnot, an' he added them to the bottom with the sheriff's phone number in case anybody wanted to make a report. Then he printed out a dozen of the posters, an' a couple plain eight-by-tens. He wished me luck on my manhunt, an' finished up with, "Don't be a stranger, Homer. I'm gettin' in a dozen new PCs next week and some dynamite new games. I could make you a real sweet deal."

I allowed as I'd give it some serious thought.

An' I aim to.

Skip Jackson

When I come outta the mission, after returnin' the reverend's pi'ture, there was a tow-headed kid sittin' on the middle of my hood. He didn't bother to git off my car as I got near, either. When I was close enough, he pointed in at the seat an' said, "That a real snake?"

"Yup." I unlocked the car door. "You got a name, young man?"

"Young man?"

"You prefer I call you boy?"

"Skip."

I shoved my hand at him. "Pleased to make your acquaintance, Skip."

He looked at me suspiciously an' made no move to shake. "Why's that?"

"Ain't every day a man gets to meet a legend."

"Legend?"

"Ain't you Skip Jackson?"

"What if I am?"

"Well, ain't many your age'd have the sense to clear out on a old man's tryin' to skin him alive, an' the savvy to find somewhere like this to hole up in 'til he's growed enough to be on his own." It was a arrangement the County Welfare'd legalized by havin' Skip declared a ward of the agency. "Takes brains," I went on. "Maybe enough you'll be runnin' the whole county one day." I could see him puffin' up at that, but he shook his head.

"You some kind of smart-ass?"

"Next to Miss Nina Ross, the smartest ass in Boone County."

"You're weird!"

I let the slur pass as I opened the car door an' removed Clyde from my seat.

"Hey!" he said. "I thought you said that was real!"

"It is." I shoved Clyde under the seat. "You didn't ask me if it was *live*." He scowled. "Only a fool'd keep a live rattler in his car." I'd known a few—gun runners an' moonshiners, mostly. One of 'em died a snakebite when he wore through his seat, an' his guard-snake bit him in the balls. But that's another story . . . "You didn't come out here to discuss my security arrangements," I said. "What can I do for you?"

He must'a decided to see it my way, 'cause he finally said, "You still lookin' for Mr. Devon?"

"I am."

"Well, there's someone might be able to tell you somethin'." I waited. "My cousin Angie. She's a friend a his."

I raised my eyebrows, an' he made a face I took to mean, "Gimme a break."

"Mr. Devon's not like that. He wouldn't hurt a kid. He's friends with most all of 'em."

"Okay. Angie here today?"

"Naw. That's the problem. She ain't been here since Mr. Devon left."

"That'd be Angie Boone?" He nodded. "The girl your older brother, Ash, is sweet on?" Again a nod. "Why do you suppose nobody's bothered to mention it to me?"

He shrugged. "Prob'ly nobody but me or Mr. Devon'd notice. Angie's sixteen. She don't have to come to school."

I got into the car but didn't start it 'til I'd rolled the window down. "Much obliged."

"Hey, can I ride in your car?"

I reckoned I owed him. I reached over an' unlocked the passenger door; he scooted round the car an' got in.

"I can only take you to the road."

He grinned as he nodded. "All right!"

By the time we got there, he'd learned how to operate the Mars lights an' the siren, an' I figgered I'd created a monster. Or, mebbe, made a friend.

ATF

My office is on the second floor of the town hall, in the northeast corner of the buildin' which is on the southwest corner of Main an' Cross. Its chief advantage is it's got windows facin' both streets, so I can keep an eye on the main drag, an' the bank, the drug store, all the in-town trouble spots, an' the post office, which is on the east side of Cross Street, without leavin' my seat. I got a comfortable chair—a semi-recliner that swivels—a desk big enough to spread my lunch out on—days I bring lunch, a chair for visitors, an' a filin' cabinet with the police radio an' a coffeepot.

When I got back from the mission, I went up to my office an' found a stranger sittin' in my chair, with his feet on my desk. He didn't rush to take 'em off when he spotted me.

"You must be the deputy sheriff," he said. He was wearin' snakeskin cowboy boots, tan slacks, a white dress shirt with no tie, a sport jacket, an' state police shades.

I nodded an' tried to keep what I thought of his manners from showin'. "An' you'd be?"

He reached into his jacket an' come out with a license wallet, which he tossed on the desk between us. "Special Agent Arnold, ATF."

I restrained the urge to ask if that was Benedict Arnold or Arnold the Pig as I picked up the wallet an' looked at it. There was a official-lookin' badge an' a officious-lookin' card that said, *George Arnold*, an' *United States Bureau of Alcohol, Tobacco and Firearms*. No picture, but the attitude was right, an' the shades were pretty much in character. I pulled my visitor's chair up to the visitor's side of my desk an' sat down. "What kin ah do fer yew, Special Agent Arnold?" I could see him fightin' to keep his sneer from showin'. Local deputy sheriffs seem to have that effect on ATF agents.

"I'm looking for one of your local good old boys," he said. "One Ash Jackson."

"What's he done?"

"Nothing that concerns you. Where will I find him?"

"Don't guess I could say. Hell, maybe."

"Don't get smart with me."

"No chance. If I was smart, I'd locked my office 'fore I went out." I put my feet on the desk an' reached behind me to open the middle drawer of my filin' cabinet an' take out my fifth of Old Grandad. I opened it an' took a swig before lookin' back at Arnold. I was pleased to note he seemed to be havin' trouble keepin' his cool an' was at a loss for somethin' to say. Finally, he put his feet on the floor an' said, "Does the sheriff approve of your drinking on the job?"

As it was plain he didn't like to be kept waitin', I took another swig an' put the bottle back in the drawer 'fore I said, "Sheriff ain't here. An' there ain't no department regulation 'gainst drinkin' on duty."

"You're pathetic! When will the sheriff be in?"

"Can't say that neither. You wanna leave a message?"

"You know what the penalty is for interfering in a federal investigation?"

"Can't say I do. You didn't say nothin' 'bout no *in*vestigation."

"I told you I'm looking for Ash Jackson."

"Duly noted. If you tell me where you're stayin' I'll let you know if he shows up. That's the best I kin do. I'd like to talk with that good ol' boy myself."

That seemed to surprise him. "What for?"

"Nothin' major. Little matter of a missin' person."

Arnold instantly lost interest. "Federal jurisdiction takes precedence." He stood up. "I'll be at the Motel Six. If you find him, I expect you to let me know immediately."

"Yes, sir!"

He started to say somethin' else, then just shook his head an' stalked out. I stayed where I was until I was sure he wasn't comin' back, then went to see which way he went. When he come out of the buildin', he climbed into a government-issue car parked on Cross Street an' drove off in the direction of Motel Six. Then I closed up my office an' went to find out from Nina what was really goin' on.

Myra Boone

When I got done talkin' to Nina—who for once didn't know as much as me—I called the hospital an' the funeral home. No luck. Then I started at the library, askin' about things in general an' Mr. Missin' Devon in particular. My big sister Alethia, who's been librarian since Ma retired to Florida, 'membered Devon. He'd been a frequent visitor to the library—'til about a month ago. I wondered out loud why I'd never run into him.

Thia said, "Maybe if you'd spend less time at the post office . . ." Thia don't entirely approve of Nina—thinks she's too young for me, an' wild.

"Don't start, Thia."

"No point," she said. "You're free, white, and twenty-one." Thia is only five-four an' skinny, but she sometimes forgets she ain't my ma.

"Not to change the subject much, but has Ash Jackson been in recently?"

"Ash Jackson has *never* been in here. Try the Sports Bar."

"I'll do that."

"What's the connection with Roger?"

I shrugged. "I'm just killin' two birds on one trip. ATF's lookin' for Ash."

"If he comes in, I'll tell him."

"Nah, don't do that. If you see him, call the sheriff."

"Anything else I can do for you?"

I held up one of the pi'tures of Devon. "You might could put up this poster," I said, knowin' my grammar'd give her fits.

She passed on the chance to correct it, an' put Devon on her bulletin board, right next to the America's Libraries READ poster of Whoopi Goldberg.

None of the clerks at Saveway had seen Devon, who I was beginnin' to think of as RD. Same went for the Baptist preacher—Reverend Nathaniel Church, an' the folks at the Shell station, the drug an' feed stores, the restaurant, an' the three in-town bars. Neither the high school bus driver nor the grammar school secretary, who knows even more than Nina 'bout what's goin' on, knew anythin'. By the most amazin' coincidence, no one I talked to could remember the last time he'd seen Ash Jackson, either. I timed my visit to the post office to coincide with the arrival of the Greyhound bus, but the driver didn't remember pickin' up anyone in Boone County since Christmas. It figured. Just to be thorough, I planned to hit the Truck Stop an' the Sports Bar, where someone should have seen Ash if not RD, but it was beginnin' to look as if Nina's guess about them was on target—Ash'd run Devon outta town, or mebbe worse, then decided to make hisself scarce 'til things cooled down.

After talkin' to the Greyhound driver, I had just enough time before supper to take a run out to the Boone place an' find out what Angie knew about it all.

The Boones have the biggest farm in the county—three hundred good acres with a blacktop drive, a two-story white house, an' a pi'ture-postcard barn. The place looked deserted. I rung the bell an' waited two or three minutes, then moseyed 'round back where the Boones parked their trucks. The backyard was blacktopped, too, an' the area between the house an' barn was ringed by farm equipment, some covered, all well kept up. There was a old-fashioned Coke machine—the kind with the little glass bottles for a quarter—next to the back door. I got outta my car an' bought a couple of Cokes. I had to open both of 'em right there, 'cause they was the kind you need a church key to get into. I half-emptied one while I looked 'round.

Mars Boone's Ford 150 was gone, but Myra's Toyota was pulled up next to the barn door, which was open. The big storage area, inside the barn, was empty, guarded by a Rottweiler big as a Kenworth tractor. He didn't bother to get up or bark when I got near, just growled a little when I got closer than he liked. There wasn't no doubt what'd happen if I crossed the line.

I went back to my car an' followed the wheel ruts from the edge of the paved yard to the dirt lane runnin' between the fields. It weren't bad, as unpaved roads go, but the squad bottomed out a couple times 'fore I got to the field where a tractor was circlin' the hay field. In the distance it looked like a Matchbox toy.

At the field gate, I stopped to watch. Myra Boone was drivin', rakin' the hay that'd probably been cut yesterday. She had on a long-sleeved shirt an' a wide-brimmed hat to keep the sun off. I got out of my car an' finished my Coke while I waited for her to come round. When she stopped an' cut the engine, I got the second Coke an' walked over. I took off my hat. "Afternoon, Miz Boone." She didn't get down, an' I had to look up to her.

"Homer." She wiped her face on her sleeve. "What brings you up this way?"

I handed her the Coke. She smiled an' took it, waitin' for a answer. I said, "One of the teachers from the mission turned up AWOL. I thought maybe Angie might'a heard 'bout it."

"Why Angie?" Myra seemed a tad alarmed.

I shrugged. "Jus' coverin' all the bases. She's the only kid I ain't talked to yet."

I thought Myra looked relieved. "She's still at school." She took a pull on the Coke bottle, then got a puzzled look on her face. "Why'n't you talk to her when you questioned the other kids?"

"I thought one of 'em tole me she wasn't there. Guess I must'a misunderstood."

"Damn straight. She goes to school every day. Else she'd be out here with me, earnin' her keep." She took a long swallow of Coke that half emptied the bottle.

I nodded again. "She mention anythin' to you about one of the teachers leavin'?"

"Nope." She finished the drink an' handed me back the bottle. "Thanks."

"You're welcome. Maybe you could have Angie stop an' see me next time she's in town?" Maybe I'd have to find Angie sooner than that. "Or gimme a call if she's heard anythin' 'bout that missin' teacher?"

"Yeah. Sure." She restarted the engine, an' whatever else she said got lost as she put it in gear.

I left the empties by the Coke machine on my way back to the road.

the Truck Stop

The sign over the pass-through from the kitchen said: EVERYONE BRINGS JOY TO THIS ESTABLISHMENT, SOME BY ENTERING, OTHERS BY LEAVING. I figured I fell into the former category, 'cause Charity Nonesuch lit up like a gambler at Las Vegas when she spotted me.

"What can I do you for, Homer?" she axed. "Coffee for openers?"

I set down at the counter. "Yes, ma'am."

The sign out front says HARDSETTER'S FOOD AND GAS, but everyone just calls it the Truck Stop. It's the best place in Boone County to eat well an' cheap. There's always half a dozen big rigs out front—a sure sign of a good place—an' Cadillacs an' New Yorkers park in b'tween the Chevys, Fords, an' GMCs. Locals from West Wheeling an' Okra drop in 'fore goin' out for a show, or bowlin', or a evenin' of power shoppin' at the Wal-Mart. Bein' a single man, I'm a fairly regular customer myself.

Charity set a steamin' mug in front of me an' waited.

"The usual, Charity," I said.

She scribbled "S&EOE" on her notepad, then put the order on the pass-through ledge. She looked 'round to see if her other customers needed her, then got herself a cup of coffee an' leaned over the counter. She's blonde, an' what I would call a generous woman, in every sense of the word.

When she leaned toward me, I got a eyeful of her generous endowments, barely contained by a tight, V-neck blouse.

"What brings you up this way?" she axed.

I took out one of the missin' man posters, which I had rolled up in my front shirt pocket, an' spread it out on the counter. "I wonder if you know this man?"

She gave me a sly grin an' said, "Wouldn't be surprised. I know most of the men in Boone County."

I knew what she meant. I had a standin' invitation, myself, to stop by her place for dessert.

Then she got serious. She took a look at Roger Devon an' shook her head. "Can't say I've seen this fella. Been missin' a month, it says here. Sad."

I said, "Yeah. It was a long shot, anyway. He's one of the Pine Ridge missionaries."

Charity pushed off from the counter an' circumnavigated the room lookin' for customers in need of refills. There were three long-haul drivers, regulars, an' a couple Okra boys in Beastie Boys shirts. When she come back, she axed, "What else is new?"

"We got a revenuer in town."

That made her prick up her ears. "Treasury man?"

"ATF."

"Am I gonna hafta drag every detail outta you?"

I shrugged. "Not much detail. He's got a badge an' a attitude, an' he's lookin' for Ash Jackson. You seen Ash lately?"

"No. Must be goin' on a month since he's been in." She didn't sound too troubled about that. "There any connection between that and this young man gone missin'?"

"There you got me, Charity. Far as I can see, there's just the timin' to connect 'em."

"And Angie Boone."

"Word does get 'round."

She blushed. “Well, Rye Willis delivers our . . . supplies.” She meant the home brew the Truck Stop kept under the counter for regular customers.

“An’ Len Hartman delivers your mail. He oughtta get extra for the newscasts.”

“He said Nina told him. She oughtta know.”

“She oughtta know better’n to pass along gossip.”

Charity ignored that. “You want I should tape this poster up on the counter by the register?”

“I’d be obliged.”

Diamond Jim

After a leisurely feed at the Truck Stop, I stopped by my house to change into my civvies an' swap the County squad for the old Dodge pickup my ma gave me when she moved away. Then I moseyed along to DJ's, West Wheeling's sports bar.

DJ's is between West Wheeling an' Okra, an' technically, outside the town boundary. It's owned by Diamond Jim Bradley, a big man—six-two an' wide as a defensive lineman—with a Cheshire cat grin. He's called Diamond Jim 'cause his taste runs to Rolexes an' diamond pinkie rings, an' he wears expensive suits an' drives a Lincoln. In spite of his substantial size, it's rumored he's a vampire 'cause he hardly ever goes out in daylight. I personally disallow such talk—no one as fond of good livin' as Jim could be such a bloodless wonder. An' whatever you say about his morals, which some compare unfavorably to a tomcat's, you gotta admit he's generous to a fault. As soon's I walked in, he was on top of me, offered to give me good odds on the playoffs, buy me a drink an' a steak dinner, an' fix me up with "a cute little number named Trixie."

When I finally convinced him I was there on business, he said, "I'm gonna figure out your price some day, Deputy. Everybody has one."

"Mebbe. But what makes you think you'd be able to afford mine?"

He laughed an' said, "I love a man with a sense of humor."

I let that go.

"Well, if I can't buy you or corrupt you, what *can* I do for you?"

I showed him my pi'ture of RD an' axed if he ever seen him. He hadn't. He hadn't seen Ash Jackson, either. By the time I'd established that Ash hadn't been by in over a week, a payin' customer'd wandered in, an' DJ hustled off to greet him. Not before he ordered the bartender—with a wink I wasn't s'posed to see—to give me a drink an' his "full cooperation."

I settled for a Lone Star. When I put two dollars on the bar, the barkeep said, "On the house. Boss's orders."

"Consider it a tip, then."

He checked to see if DJ was watchin', then pocketed the bills. When he moved down the bar to take another order, he took RD's pi'ture along. In a few minutes, one of the bar's regulars pushed his MGD down the bar toward me an' said, "Hear you're lookin' for Ash Jackson."

I said, "That's right. Seen him?"

"No, but I saw his truck over in Okra. Out front of Calamity Jane's."

"Sure it was Ash's truck?"

"Big, new, shiny, black 250, with mudders an' a beefed up suspension, a blue garter on the rearview, a Landoll in the back window, an' a bumper sticker that says: INSURED BY SMITH & WESSON?"

"That's it. How long ago?"

"A week, maybe."

Calamity Jane's

The town of Okra's a kinda white-trash poor relation to West Wheeling. It's closer to the interstate an' the city, so it tends to filter out most of the rough trade an' riffraff 'fore they get down our way. It's got a XXX-rated movie house an' a strip joint, but also a first-rate steak house—you take the good with the rest.

Calamity Jane's is a Country an' Western bar on the northeast side, a place where—rumor has it—they don't think highly of the Law. It's also out of my jurisdiction. I was countin' on not bein' recognized without my uniform. My cover story was that Roger Devon owed me money, an' I'd pay ten bucks to find out where to collect. I also held out that Ash Jackson had insulted my sister an' I was gunnin' for him as well. To make it look like I was fixin' to wait all night if necessary, I fed a handful of quarters to the jukebox an' sucked down a couple of beers.

I had plenty of time to study the place. It had "real" C&W atmosphere—most of which was home-rolled. The restrooms were labeled BULLS an' HEIFERS, an' there was a brass footrail on the bar, a pair of long horns over the door to the back room, an' spittoons scattered 'round in corners. Half a dozen local hustlers was passin' the same twenty around over a pool table in the back. Two old codgers was playin' checkers under a wagon wheel chandelier, an' a older woman, sittin' at the bar, was drinkin' herself into oblivion.

I played Dolly an' Reba 'til they started soundin' the same, an' the Old Style was givin' me a hangover without givin' me a buzz. The evenin' was startin' to look wasted.

Then a couple of rowdies come in spoilin' for a fight. One was the perfect urban cowboy, down to his snakeskin boots an' matchin' vest. He started it, puttin' a arm around the older lady. When he tried to kiss her, the bartender got in the act.

"Get the hell out!"

"What's she to you, Joe, your sister?"

Joe hitched his thumb toward the door. "Beat it!"

"Sez who?" the cowboy demanded.

The second rowdy sneered, "Him an' his army."

Cowboy held up his right fist. "His right army . . ." Then his left. ". . . Or his left army?"

Joe started down the bar to where, I s'pected, he kept his equalizer stowed. The second rowdy must'a been thinkin' the same thing, 'cause he vaulted over the bar to head him off.

I looked around. The hustlers had put down their sticks an' was watchin' the show. Nobody else in the place seemed either sober enough to get what was goin' on or inclined to give a damn. So *I* butted in.

I stood up an' swayed like a drunk. "Shay. Joe. 'Bout another . . . ?" I let it trail off, like I forgot what to say. That done the trick. I had everybody's attention. I leaned over the bar an' delivered a *di*versionary left hook to the second rowdy's jaw, then a hard right to his solar plexus. He dropped like Wile E. Coyote when he'd run outta cliff.

The cowboy's mouth fell open. "Who the hell are you?"

I grinned. "I'm the Marines," I said 'fore I decked him.

Joe didn't waste no time draggin' the second rowdy out from behind the bar, right out to the parkin' lot.

I grabbed Cowboy under the armpits an' called out, "Anybody know what these good ol' boys is drivin'?"

One of the checker players grinned at me. He looked two years older than dirt an' was missin' his teeth. "Rusty Ford with the camper an' the sign that says: WIFE AND DOG MISSING—REWARD FOR DOG."

Joe an' I agreed that neither of our new friends was in fit shape to drive home, so we relieved 'em of their keys—which we hid in their own glove box—an' left 'em sleepin' it off in the back of their truck.

Back inside, Joe broke out a bottle of the good stuff an' poured me a double shot "on the house." He poured hisself one an' we toasted "the Marines."

After we'd had a chance to savor the liquor, he said, "You lookin' for work nights?"

"Thanks, but no thanks."

He nodded. "Just a thought." After another wait, he said, "Dan Underhill might know somethin' about Ash."

"Where'll I find *him?*"

"He'll be in around eleven."

Dan Underhill turned out to be someone I knew—on sight, if not by name. *He* was outta uniform, too, but I recognized him quick enough, even without his mirror shades. He was one of the stone-faced state troopers—AKA "The Sergeant"—that I do business with regular. Joe introduced us formal.

"Dan, this here's my friend," he told Underhill. "—What'd you say your name is?" he axed me.

"Vergil." I wanted to say "Tibbs" but decided against it—in case Joe was a movie buff. "Vergil Smith."

Underhill managed to keep his face straight.

Out of uniform—an' with me vouched for by my new best

friend—"Dan" was a regular guy. My C&W disguise hadn't fooled him for a minute, but he was decent enough not to blow my cover. An' he was pleased I was lookin' for Ash.

"Something you can lock him up for?"

"Don't get your hopes up."

He seemed hopeful anyway as I explained about our missin' person, then he shook his head.

" 'Bout ten days ago, I had an unofficial complaint. Guy *hadn't* seen Ash, but a few days before that he'd seen Ash's truck in the lot, here, right before last call. He noticed a girl sittin' in it, young an' a looker. He wanted to buy her a drink, but the guy he was with recognized the truck an' warned him Ash was trouble, even if the girl didn't turn out to be jailbait. So this fella went about his business, but the more he thought about it, the madder he got, especially with Ash not bein' an Okran. Since my informant's married, he decided to let it go an' just tell me. I've been watchin' for Ash, but he hasn't been back."

Later, I tracked down Underhill's informant, who described Angie Boone to a *T*.

Ash Jackson's

Andrew "Ash" Jackson got his name from the rumor his old man killed the ash tree growin' out in their front yard by cuttin' switches off it to use on Ash. Ash's only visible means of support was a occasional odd job of the sort that's short on effort an' long on financial gain. An' he weren't known to be particular about ethics or legal niceties. He was such a good liar, he even fooled me sometimes, but he had so little respect for other people's intelligence, he didn't bother keepin' his stories straight. If he had, he'd a been dangerous.

Since nobody I'd axed about him'd seen him, I figured a little visit to his place would be in order. It's out off County C, a half mile south of the east-west interstate. I headed out right after breakfast. The driveway's a quarter mile long, unpaved dirt, just wheel ruts separated by foot-tall grass. The grass cleaned off the bottom of my car real well by the time I pulled up to the door.

I sat in the car a while. Ash claimed to live alone, an' his truck weren't there, but just in case he had relatives stayin', I wanted to give 'em time to git ready for visitors. Folks in these parts are the soul of hospitality, but they don't take kindly to surprises. An' they all have guns.

The house'd been white once, prob'ly 'fore Ash was born. It was a small, wood frame affair with a porch across the whole front, shaded by the roof overhang. The house faces north, an' moss completely covered the roof, which'd been shingled, but so long ago you couldn't tell what color it'd been. After about five minutes, by which time I'd taken note of everythin' there was to notice in the front, I got out an' moseyed up to the front door. No one answered when I knocked. By this time, I was pretty sure no one would. The grass in the drive didn't seem to have been disturbed in some time, an' there weren't any other signs of recent activity. Ash must'a been outta town.

There wasn't any fence or NO TRESPASSING signs around, so I sauntered 'round back, lookin' in all the windows that didn't have the shades pulled. Inside, I could see a big-screen TV an' a state-of-the-art CD/stereo. Out back was a satellite dish. On the back porch under the eaves, in a padlocked cage welded together out of rebar, there was a gas-powered generator to run the equipment when County Power's lines was down. Ash wasn't doin' too bad.

I went back to the front an' left a note shoved between the screen door an' the jamb. It said, ASH, LOOK ME UP ASAP. DEPUTY SHERIFF DETERS

Rye Willis

Time I got back to County C, I was sure Rye knew more about Ash an' the missin' missionary than he'd been givin' hisself credit for, so I decided to go straight to the horse's mouth an', if necessary, stick my flashlight down his throat. Rye's place is as far out in the sticks as Ash Jackson's, only on the other side of West Wheeling, so it took me the better part of an hour to get there. I ignored both the NO TRESPASSING sign an' the one that said, TRESPASSERS WILL BE VIOLATED.

Mrs. Willis, Rye's ma, was hangin' the wash out when I pulled up in the yard. I took my time gettin' out of the car so—in case there was anythin' lyin' around I shouldn't see—they'd have time to get it outta sight. The house was as old an' the same style as Ash's, but newly painted an' freshly shingled. There was a round table an' two Adirondack chairs on the porch.

When I finally come up to her, Mrs. Willis nodded an' said, "Mornin', Sheriff." She kept clippin' the clothes onto the line with spring pins. "This a social call?"

"Not exactly, Ma'am. I need to talk to Rye."

"You gonna arrest him?"

"Not if he cooperates."

She sighed an' said, "I'll get 'im." She walked over to the porch an' hefted a twenty-two that was leanin' against the front doorjamb, an' fired three shots into the ground. She put the gun back an' said, "Might as well set an' wait. Can I get you somethin'?"

I sat on one of the Adirondack chairs. "I'd be obliged for a drink of water."

She nodded an' went in the house. She come back with a tall, cold glass. The Willises have a well with the sweetest water in the state. If they ever lose the recipe for shine, they could make a fortune sellin' their water to city folks an' yuppies. I said, "Much obliged," an' drained the glass an' give it back to her.

She set it on the table. "I got to get back to work. Rye'll be along directly."

He was. I saw his head poke out from behind one of the outbuildings, then disappear. Shortly afterward, he come out of the house with a brown an' tan gallon jug an' a glass. "What brings you out this way, Homer?" He poured his glass an' my empty one half full from the jug, an' picked up his glass. "Here's to old friends an' good likker."

I picked up my glass an' nodded, an' we both had a swig. It was some of his best stuff an' it burned down to my tailbone. Then I proposed another toast. "An' friends who don't hold out on friends."

I thought he went a shade pale, but it could'a been the sun goin' behind a cloud just then. He did look plenty uncomfortable. "Aw, Homer, you know I wouldn't—" He slugged down the rest of his shine.

I sipped mine an' let him squirm a little while the likker done its work. Better'n truth serum, Rye's brew. He refilled his glass an' topped mine off.

Finally I said, "I ain't sayin' what you tole me weren't the truth, Rye, but it sure weren't the whole truth." I leaned towards him an' lowered my voice. "I need to know what happened to that missionary fella."

This time, I was sure he went whiter. He swallowed an' said, "Ash'll kill me."

"You're gonna have to decide if you're more scared of Ash or me."

"Well, Homer, worst I figger you'll do to me is shut me down . . ."

I could see his point. Ash mightn't be so forgivin'. So I hung a carrot in front of his nose. "How 'bout if I treat what you tell me as confidential? Ash wouldn't have to know less'n we haul him into court on murder charges, an' we won't do that unless we're sure we got 'im." Then I showed him the stick. I said, real softly, "You know you want to be cooperative with the Law, Rye." I didn't have to mention his business'd suffer if he wasn't.

Rye looked like his best horse just foundered. I let him think about it long as he needed.

Finally, he said, "Ash told me the missionary fella was turnin' Angie Boone agin him, fillin' her head with funny ideas. He said he was gonna run 'im outta the state."

The way Rye looked at me when he stopped talkin', I could tell he was figgerin' whether or not I'd buy that that was all there was to it. I said, "Rye, you ain't even *close* to a decent liar, so don't waste my time tryin'. Just gimme the facts."

He let out a big sigh, then got on with it. "He made me go with him to the mission that night, made me wait in his truck while he went in to *per*suade the missionary fella to get outta town. After a while, I see the guy's car pull up next to the truck. Ash's in the passenger seat, an' the missionary fella's drivin'. Ash tells me to follow 'em, an' we *pro*ceed back to his place, where my truck's parked."

Rye stopped an' said, "I gotta have another drink."

"You gotta finish your story first."

"Yeah. Well, that's all there is."

I waited.

"We get to Ash's. He tells me I can go. So, I went. I never seen that missionary fella again, an' I ain't seen Ash recent, neither."

"If Devon," I said, usin' the missin' man's name for the first time in our conversation, "was alive an' well when you last seen him, Rye, how come you're so damn jumpy?"

"I didn't see nothin', mind you. When we get to his place, Ash tells me what happens next is none of my business an' to get lost. So I get in my truck an' drive off." There was more; I waited. Rye finally got to it. "Just about the time I get back to County C, I hear a shot. Just one.

"Sounded like Ash's old Winchester."

Grandpa

"Grandpa, if you was tryin' to make someone disappear in the county, where'd you put him?"

Grandpa gave me a funny look, then shrugged an' said, "Mine." He meant one of the dozen abandoned mines hereabouts.

"What I figured, too. Where else?"

"Goode Swamp." It took him a lot of breath to say that much, but he weren't done.

I tried to help out. "If I was tryin' to make his car disappear, too, I'd drop it somewheres off Car Wrecks."

Grandpa nodded, meanin' his whole upper body swayed forward an' back.

"Thanks, Grandpa." He nodded again, just his head this time, an' held up his coffee mug.

I said, "Name your poison."

"Coffee."

I half filled the mug an' put in milk an' two sugars like he liked.

He croaked, "Obliged."

I waited 'til he'd had a slug.

He said, "Sump'n else?"

"Yes, sir."

"Sir, hunh. What'd you want?"

I figured I might as well get it over with, so I just spit it out.

"I'd like your permission to court Miss Nina, sir."

Grandpa made a sound like, "Humph." Then he started to shake like he was havin' some kind of fit, then he started on a coughin' jag, an' I knew he was laughin' his head off. I just stood there an' waited 'til he got his breath an' hauled out his bandanna. He wiped the tears from his eyes an' hawked into it an' put it back in his pocket. When he started to answer me, he started laughin' again, an' it was some time 'fore I could make out what he was sayin'.

"Boy, if you're fool enough to try courtin' Nina, God help you. I sure as hell ain't gonna get in yer way."

Car Wrecks

Car Wrecks is a two-mile stretch of county highway runnin' along our local river, which is a tad wild at that point with zigzags an' ten or fifteen streams feedin' it by way of ravines an' steep-sided gullies. The half of 'em that the road crosses have bridges of one sort an' another. Between the zigzags an' the bridges, there's plenty chance for careless or suicidal drivers to kill theirselves; plenty of 'em take it. An' with all of it, there's plenty places a car can go off the road an' never be found. Over the years, killers an' car thieves've learned to take advantage of this handy feature. I guessed that if Roger Devon'd disappeared by accident, suicide, or murder, there was a good chance it was into Car Wrecks. So after talkin' to Rye an' Grandpa, I had lunch, then got a rope an' my binoculars an' headed out there. I decided to be systematic; I started at the end closest to Ash's place.

After a month, most of the clear signs of a car goin' off the road'd be gone. The trees had leafed out; grass had growed taller; the couple good storms we'd had had washed any tracks away. Huntin' for a wreck consisted of parkin' my squad where it'd be least likely to get hit, an' walkin' along the shoulder with my field glasses lookin' for man-made stuff down in the gullies. Every time I spotted somethin' I couldn't identify, I'd climb down for a look-see. To make things easier next time I hadda do a search, I hauled a lot of stuff up to the road. It was hot an' dusty work. My knees an' knuckles got skinned, an' my uniform was trashed. It took me two hours to go just half a mile, coverin' only the north side of the road. I'd just crossed to the south side an' started back toward my car when I spotted somethin' large an' gray, an' mostly hid by brush down below.

It was a old gray Escort. I spotted the Ford logo 'fore I was halfway down the slope. The car was in pretty good shape considerin' how fast it must've been goin' to end up so far from the road, an' that it'd fell eighteen feet. It obviously hadn't caught fire, an' the side windows—I could see 'em as I slid down—were unbroke. I was happy to find there was nobody inside. No body. But the windshield had blowed out all over the crumpled hood, so there *could* be some remains around somewhere. I looked, though I wasn't sure what I expected to find. If there had been a body a month ago, it could still be around somewhere, some of it. Or it could'a been et by critters—bears, or coyotes, coons, or local dogs. If there weren't no body, it could be 'cause Roger Devon—at this point I had no doubt it was *his* car—had totaled it, by accident or on purpose, or 'cause someone else'd dumped it to hide RD's disappearance. There was too many possibilities. An' 'fore any of 'em could be checked out, the car'd have to be processed an' the area searched for remains.

I decided to call for reinforcements.

Lotta times, when a vehicle ends up in Car Wrecks, we don't bother to haul it out. Draggin' a couple tons of crushed metal straight up the twenty-foot side of a ravine just ain't worth it for salvage. Mostly we diagram the location, take lots of pi'tures, an' notify the *in*surance company involved where they can go see what's left. Then we forgit it. Either the *ve*hicle rusts in peace an' into pieces, or local entrepreneurs take what they can pry loose for parts an' scrap. Either way, it ain't much of a problem for me.

That weren't the case with Devon's Escort. I started by callin' Martha Rooney on the radio an' axin' her to run the car plates. When she come back that it *was* Devon's car, I axed her to send out Nina with my camera, an' have the State Police send a evidence man, an' Truck Towing send their biggest rig. Martha wanted all the details, but I tole her I'd let her know later—too many locals amuse theirselves by listenin' to scanners. While I waited for Nina, I went back an' got my car. I left it up above the wreck with the motor runnin' an' the lights on. Then I got out the crime-scene tape an' stretched it along the road to mark off-limits for the rubberneckers I knew'd be showin' up soon.

I was right about that. A good two dozen cars was on the scene 'fore the first state car. Then three of 'em showed—it was a slow day for crime on the interstate. I had the troopers run the gawkers off, while I went back down an' took pi'tures of the wreck. When the crime scene guy showed up, I had 'im go over the outside of the Escort for fingerprints, blood, or anythin' else of interest. By the time he was done, Dwayne Truck arrived with the rig he uses for disabled semis. He didn't have enough cable to run all the way down the ravine, so we had to wait while he sent for more. Meanwhile, three of the troopers an' Nina an' me fanned out from the wreck lookin' for a body. All we got for our trouble was scratches an' *ex*posure to poison oak.

"You could hide a dozen bodies in this mess," Nina said, finally. "Why don't you get Martha to call for a trackin' dog?"

"Sounds like a plan to me," I said, an' did.

Patrick Truck showed up shortly thereafter with a hundred-foot cable an' another truck. It was good he did. It was a good thing, too, that I'd taken lots of pi'tures, 'cause by the time they'd dragged that poor Escort back up on the road, its undercarriage was damn near battered off, an' the side of the ravine had relocated south.

'Bout the time I sent one of the troopers off with the Escort to guard it at Truck's Garage, the dog showed up, a prize-winnin' bloodhound named Holmes. We hoisted him an' his handler down the ravine. Holmes took off, bayin', an' we all followed—over to the river an' back. He treed a coon, dug a rattler out from under a log, an' led Nina an' me an' the two remainin' troopers on a merry chase. Kept us all goin' 'til sundown.

We never found a hair of Roger Devon.

truck towing

My friend Dwayne could rebuild a engine with a screwdriver an' a crescent wrench. He's never run from a fight or let a friend down. He don't drink or cuss, an' I'd bet a year's pay he's never cheated on his wife. A good man.

After the old United Transit Corp went belly up owin' their help a month's back wages, Dwayne found himself outta work. Fortunately, he an' his brothers'd saved a little an' were able to buy up Call'N Haul, the local towin' outfit, which they renamed Truck Towing. Dwayne had a mechanic's lien on most of United Transit's equipment, 'cause of the money owed him, an' he went to court an' got the titles. Then, 'cause the county had to have busses to get the kids to school, the bank board of directors voted to give Truck Towing a loan to buy the UTC property an' a few old GMC coaches. Dwayne hired his wife an' sisters to drive 'em while he an' his brothers kept 'em up. It all worked out. The long an' the short of it is, Truck Transit and Towing is a goin' concern with some of the best lookin' drivers this side of either coast.

RD's car was so banged up by the time they got it outta the ravine, they'd had to put it on a flatbed truck to get it back to the shop. There, Dwayne off-loaded it into the shed the county uses for a evidence *im*pound.

By the time *I* got there, Trooper Yates, the state evidence guy, was packin' up. He was dirty an' scratched from crawlin' around the wreck down in the ravine, an' pretty much disgusted by his lack of progress back at TT&T.

"Least you could'a come up with a body for as much trouble as this was," he tole me.

"Yessir. I know just how you feel."

After he left, I had a look at the Escort, which was sittin' in the shed with its trunk open an' its hood off—they'd had to remove it to get at the engine. The missin' windshield had been replaced with a plastic sheet, taped up top with duct tape an' pulled down over the engine compartment. The inside of the car was covered in places with gray smudges that looked like smeared fingerprints—which they was.

I made a note of what I seen, includin' that the seat'd been moved from where it was when we found the car. Since I didn't know how RD usually kept his seat adjusted, the observation didn't do no good. There wasn't much of anythin' else to see. Devon kept his car pretty clean inside—in spite of Trooper Yates's claim of "enough dirt to plant potatoes in." There hadn't been no empty coffee cups or fast-food leftovers. The trunk had the usual stuff—jack, tire iron an' spare, a few railroad fuses, an' a dead flashlight. There wasn't no trace of the stuff the Reverend Moody said Devon took with him when he left.

I turned off the light an' was lockin' up when Dwayne come by.

"You're stayin' for supper."

Dwayne's got three inches an' sixty pounds on me, so I wasn't gonna argue. Besides, his wife's a great cook. I got out the spare uniform I keep in my trunk for emergencies, an' went into the garage. Dwayne's got a little office in front, with a TV an' a couch that mostly only his huntin' dogs use. The office has a powder room that's not too unsanitary for public use. I used it to wash up an' change. As we cut through the shop to get to the house, I noticed Dwayne had a new sign hung over the door:

	<u>CUSTOMARY CHARGES</u>
LABOR	$17.50/hour
IF YOU WATCH	$25.00/hour
IF YOU HELP	$50.00/hour
IF YOU WORKED ON IT BEFORE YOU BROUGHT IT IN	FORGET IT!

I wondered who'd worked on Roger Devon's car.

mining for bodies

Most of the operators of our local micro-distilleries use abandoned mines to store their products, an' like all good businessmen, they take precautions against break-ins. So 'fore I went pokin' around, I went to find Rye Willis. I tracked him down at the Truck Stop, before sunup, an' watched him unload twenty cases of "West Wheeling White Vinegar" at the back door. White Lightning would have been more accurate labelin', but I didn't guess anybody'd complain to the FDA. Me watchin' made him nervous.

Rye knows the mine territory as well as his back porch but when I explained what I wanted, he was reluctant to get involved. "You're workin' with the ATF!"

"I'm lookin' for a missin' person, Rye, but if I have to get that ATF clown to bird-dog your booby traps, I'll do it."

"Homer, I'm shocked!"

"Yeah. An' I'm a virgin."

"Don't do it, Homer. ATF agents're like those brooms in *Fantasia*—kill one, thirty more pop up in his place."

"Guess you'd better help me then, eh, Rye?"

We started just after sunrise an' took Merlin 'cause Rye wanted him to keep his hand in as a tracker. We stopped at the Truck Stop for breakfast an' hit the first mine shaft before the dew burnt off the grass. It made two days in a row I'd had to get out of my car an' exercise. My job was gettin' to be more like work. Speakin' of which, Rye told me there was thirty-two abandoned mines in the county. Fortunately, we didn't have to stick our heads into the mouths of every one. Two of the places were so remote no one from outside the county could've found 'em, an' no local'd go to the trouble of haulin' *anythin'* that far away. The roads leadin' to a few were overgrown with three-inch or better saplings. It was a fair bet no one had visited *them* in the last month.

We covered eighteen likely body dumpin' spots by noon, an' had lunch at the nineteenth—Rye's private warehouse. Merlin would've bailed out at that point only, as I was drivin' an' told him he'd have to walk back, he elected to stay the course.

We headed out to a scrub-covered ridge that had a mine with a main entry an' half a dozen air shafts you could've squeezed a corpse down. It looked promisin' for a dump site—vehicles had been passin' often an' recent enough to keep the access road open an' the grass flat between the wheel ruts. We piled outta the car an' spread out, Rye an' me goin' one way, Merlin the other. Climbin' across the side slope of the ridge would've been hard goin' enough, but we was also workin' up a lather pushin' through thickets of thumb-sized trees an' waist-high brambles. I was ready to call the hunt off when Merlin yelled out, "Hey, I found a body!"

Rye an' me set some kind of land speed record gettin' up to the ridge top where Merlin was standin'. Below him, in a little hollow where the underbrush thinned on a patch of rocky ground, lay a skeleton with its bleached bones in near perfect arrangement to where they'd been in life. I stared for a minute, then heaved a sigh of relief. The bones wasn't human. I said, "I'll be damned."

Rye said, "Merlin, you jackass! You made us run all the way up here for a dead dog?"

Merlin laughed. "You said we was lookin' for a missing body. What's that there if it ain't a body? An' missin'?"

Rye looked ready to pop him one, so I got between 'em. "He's got a point, Rye. 'Sides, this may just clear up another missin' person case I've had hangin' fire."

"Don't *you* try an' pull my leg, Homer!"

"Seriously," I said, " 'less I'm mistaken, that there's the remains of Marge Wexler."

Rye grinned. "Miz Wexler's a dog, Homer, but c'mon!"

I laughed; I couldn't help myself. Merlin didn't get it, so I explained.

"Everybody in Boone County knows Axel's wife's a bitch an' that she run off a while back. Most nobody knows her name—it's Maybelle. *Marge* was Axel's prize huntin' dog. He never filed a missin' person report for Maybelle, but I still got one outstandin' that he filed when the dog went gone."

Merlin grinned, too. "So what're you gonna do, bring Axel up here for a look?"

What he meant was that the circumstances surroundin' the dog's death was plain to see. The skeleton lay on its side with what was left of a red leather collar in the region of its neck. The collar was attached to one end of a twenty-foot chain; a hunk of one-by-eight siding was stapled to the other end. The siding end of the chain was jammed between a sapling an' a rock, an' wrapped tight enough around the tree to bite into the trunk. Plain to see, the dog'd broke the board loose from the shed she'd been chained to an' headed cross country, trailin' board an' chain. When she snagged the board between the tree an' rock, she'd run around the tree an' really got herself stuck. Then she'd starved to death waitin' for rescue.

"I'm gonna handle this with the same dignity an' respect I would any missin' person case," I said. "With the exception, I don't think we need to notify the state *po*lice." That caused 'em to grin. "If you boys'll just give me a hand . . ."

So I got my camera an' stuff outta the car, an' took a roll of pi'tures of the bones—*in situ,* as we say in law enforcement, first from the ridge, then up close—an' the chain, collar, an' tree. Then the three of us carefully put all them bones in a gunny sack, an' the sack—with the collar an' chain—in a box in my trunk.

We finished checkin' out the last of the mines near sundown. We didn't find no other body.

the body in Goode Swamp

Goode Swamp got its name from Samuel Goode, the first white man on record to disappear into one of its quicksand traps. By all accounts he was purely a lowlife an' no loss. If a swamp is a soggy spot full of snakes, bugs, an' varmints, Goode Swamp's a winner. For openers, it's got every type of reptile ever seen in these parts—most of 'em poison—an' every crawlin' critter that ever made men miserable, from ants an' chiggers to skeeters an' ticks. Of course there's four-legged varmints, too—skunks, coons, possum, an' black bear. I even heard stories of gators, but I think they're confusin' Goode Swamp with the New York sewers. Of course the most vexin' an' dangerous variety of swamp life is the two-legged kind—gun runners, trappers, an' your occasional escaped convict. I wasn't aware of any of the last category around lately, but the first sort was a constant threat. Which is why I pressed Rye into service as a guide the mornin' after our little minin' expedition.

"Homer, why are we doin' this?"

" 'Cause we already looked in all the easy spots. An' this is the world's best place to lose a body."

"That bein' the case, why are we botherin' to search at all?"

"We gotta show we made a effort. Once we establish we can't find nothin', we can quit."

"You talk just like a politician."

"I gotta get in practice—in case Sheriff Rooney should decide to retire."

When we was loadin' Rye's aluminum canoe, an' our waders in the back of my truck, Rye pointed to the sticker on the bumper that said, "THEY GOT THE LIBRARY AT ALEXANDRIA BUT THEY'RE NOT GETTING MINE."

"Homer, I been meanin' to ask—what the hell does that mean?"

My ma put the sticker on the truck when she was West Wheeling librarian. "The library of Alexandria was one of the wonders of the world 'til they burned it down."

"Recently?"

I had to smile. "Naw."

"Why'd they burn it down?"

I thought about tryin' to explain ancient history to a guy who never finished eighth grade—not that he ain't smart. I gave it up an' said, "Drunks. Mean drunks." Rye could relate to mean drunks. I guessed, from the look on his face, that he didn't entirely get it but was afraid he'd look stupid if he axed any more, so I switched to a subject he knew somethin' about. "So, Rye. How many two-legged varmints you reckon call Goode Swamp home?"

" 'Pends on what you mean by varmints."

We stopped for breakfast at the Truck Stop, where the subject of the day's gossip was Roger Devon's car. After I assured everybody I couldn't possibly know as much about it as they did—me bein' only the deputy sheriff—they let us eat in peace. Charity was good enough to put us up some fried chicken, 'fore we left, in a Styrofoam cooler.

Twenty minutes after we was outta the Truck Stop, we turned onto Goode Swamp Road. We bumped along it 'til I thought my fillings'd fall out. Rye's head kept swivelin' to the back like a owl's as he tried to keep an eye on the case of white lightnin' he'd brought along to trade an', at the same time, look ahead for signs that anyone'd been along recent.

The road changed—from blacktop to gravel, then dirt as it dropped into Goode Hollow, an' the trees changed—from hardwoods to stands of willows an' cottonwoods as the ground got wetter, with more an' more giant poplars an' pin oaks.

The dirt road run along a creek that widened into a pond so clogged with cattails you could scarcely see the water. Just about the point where the road petered out, Rye tole me to stop the truck an' wait while he went to check somethin'. I thought he meant the plumbin' until he hauled out one of his jugs of shine. He was gone a good forty-five minutes. I used the time to slather on bug dope 'til I smelled like Lysol, an' watch a hawk drift by overhead. Just for my entertainment, a family of muskrats swum out in the pond, an' a couple of red-winged blackbirds cussed at each other across their mutual boundary. A heron stalked out of the cattails, froze for a minute, then snagged its lunch. A squirrel started across the clearin' where the road'd been before it disappeared. He spotted me an' changed his mind in midair, then disappeared back into the scrub.

When I got bored with the free show, I checked the loads in my .38, then tested the batteries in the flashlight I keep in the glove box. Rye openin' the passenger door suddenly scared near two years off my life.

"Dammit, Rye. Don't do that!"

He made a Do-What? face but couldn't play innocent long. He was bustin' to tell me what he'd learnt.

"I just found out somebody was through here 'bout a month ago—went back out lighter'n they went in."

"Who?"

"My informant couldn't say."

"Couldn't or wouldn't?"

"He never seen 'em—just their tracks. Figured they must'a been up to no good—illegal dumpin', mebbe."

"What's this informant's name?"

"I promised not to tell."

I gave Rye a look, an' he said, "Oh, all right. Charlie Reelfoot. But you didn't get that from me."

I'd heard of Charlie. Not someone I'd like to have testify in court, but likely he knew his swamp. "What'd he say about who these mysterious strangers was that he didn't see?"

"Said he guessed it was a man an' boy—from the tracks."

It could have been Ash an' one of his younger brothers. I wondered what Skip'd been doin' the night this all went down, an' would he tell me what he knew if Ash or he was in on it. Somethin' to look into.

So I fished out my county ordnance map an' put Clyde's cousin, Maude, on the seat of the truck. We locked it, an' put our lunch an' waders, the rest of the white lightnin', an' my camera an' radio in the canoe.

We headed downstream. It took us a hour paddlin', an' fightin' our way through weeds an' under tree branches to get to a place we could've drove to if Rye's informant'd been a tad more helpful. The streambed widened out an' was crossed by a ford some civic-minded local'd improved with a truckload of crushed rock.

I said, "Rye, why'n hell didn't you tell me about this?"

"I didn't *know,* Homer. Or you think I woulda let us come all this way . . . ?"

"Why the hell didn't Charlie tell you?"

"Guess 'cause I didn't ask." He shrugged. "This must be where Ash an' his buddy dumped him."

"Devon?"

"That's who we're lookin' for, ain't it?"

"Yeah. Let's get on with it."

We grounded the canoe, an' I located where we was on the ordnance map.

"Charlie said 'bout the length of a tanker truck sun-side of the ford." Rye pointed south. "That way."

I rolled up the map, slung the camera round my neck an' clipped the radio on my belt. The two of us started workin' our way downstream. Maybe fifty yards past the ford, the water was deep an' fast runnin'. After more'n a month, there weren't no tracks left, but the feel of the place fit the scenario we was workin' off of. I looked back at the ford an' axed Rye, "Sure Charlie didn't mean a tanker convoy?"

"He may've. He ain't had much education. What're we gonna do now?"

We unloaded the canoe an' carried it around the ford, then reloaded it an' started downriver. I felt like I was in a West Wheeling version of *Deliverance*, only instead of duelin' banjos, we had duelin' red-wing blackbirds, an' in place of yahoo locals we had to watch for cottonmouths an' skeeters carryin' encephalitis. Instead of searchin' for our disappearin' youths, we was lookin' for a missin' person.

Still, the sun was warm an' golden where it filtered through the trees, an' the smells an' sounds of the river made you think of birth an' death an' all life's beauty. I was struck by the notion that city folks work all their lives to retire to places like this.

Rye must've been thinkin' along the same lines, 'cause he said, "It don't get much better'n this."

"All we need is some cold beers an' a couple fishin' poles."

"Speakin' of cold, I wish we had some ice."

"I believe we do." I got out the lunch Charity'd made us. Tucked away between the ice cubes an' the foil-wrapped chicken was cans of Classic Coke. Bless that woman.

As we moved along, we kept our eyes on the riverbanks for places where a body might've washed or been dragged ashore. I spotted a snake as big around as Nina's ankles an' said, "Rye, what's worse'n seein' a cottonmouth on your trail?"

"Not seein' 'im." We both laughed. Rye said, "Homer, I think you should pay me for this trip."

"Why's that?"

"If I was servin' jury duty, I'd get fifteen dollars a day."

"Yeah, but you wouldn't get to bring your white lightnin' along to peddle."

"Wanna bet?"

"Okay. I'll pay you fifteen dollars."

"For yesterday, too?"

"You drive a hard bargain."

Rye grinned. We slowed to check a turn in the stream where floatin' trash collected. We were both relieved not to find any bodies. Rye's comment was, "Looks like we might've lucked out here, Homer." After a few more minutes he axed, "How're we gonna get back to the truck?"

"I'm workin' on— What the hell . . . ?"

Rye spotted the "what" an' said, "Dammit!"

The *what* was just below the water surface, on the inside of a meander where the stream slowed an' the bank sloped gradual. It was just big enough that there was no mistakin' the white curve of it—bone. It was without doubt part of a skull. Rye, who was in the front of the canoe, steered it closer to the shore.

I said, "Don't disturb the bottom 'til I get pi'tures." I unpacked my camera an' checked the date setting.

Rye swung the boat around so I could snap a few, then paddled back to midstream. "Now what?"

I been to police academy an' been trained on how to secure crime scenes. The course didn't cover what to do when your crime scene is a *en*tire swamp. I decided to let the state cops handle it. "I think we'll get some backup, startin' with the state *po*lice."

I picked up the radio an' raised Martha Rooney, told her to send in the cavalry.

While we waited, we carefully doped out what'd happened, an' searched the riverbanks on both sides for remains. We found a nearly perfect footprint, half filled with a month's settlin' of silt. It told the tale. The body'd washed downstream to the meander, where it floated near shore in the lessened current. A black bear'd found it an' drug it up on the bank. There were bits an' bones scattered over an acre, all of 'em gnawed clean an' polished. There was no clothes or fingerprints or teeth. It was a hell of a crime scene. I wasn't sure where to begin.

The state cops weren't a whole lot clearer on the subject. They come upriver by boat from a popular launchin' spot near the road. The man in charge turned out to be Dan Underhill. He kept a perfectly straight face as he took in the situation, then said, "Looks like your missing man kinda went to pieces, Deputy."

picking up the pieces

"What we got here," I said, "is a probable homicide—no body. Seems our victim an' scene are spread out all over Goode Swamp."

Rye didn't say nothin'. Underhill snorted.

Trooper Yates looked disgusted. "What's wrong with an old-fashioned murder, where a couple of good old boys get liquored up and shoot each other, or stomp somebody to death? With a nice, tidy scene. Indoors somewhere? This—" He waved his arm around. "Is criminal!"

"Yessir," I said.

We decided not to make a federal case of it. We took "before" pi'tures of everythin' 'til I was beginnin' to wish I had stock in Kodak. Then we marked off the "scene"—what wasn't underwater—with strings, in a grid pattern, an' diagrammed an' measured the location of every bit of our victim. Since we had to write everythin' down, it took a long time. Then we took a second set of pi'tures of the scene with markers—we used paper cups with numbers wrote on 'em with Magic Marker 'cause that's what we had on hand.

Not long after we started, Trooper Yates stopped an' shook his head. "Grizzly."

"No," Rye told him, "it was black bears."

When we'd pretty much got the scene processed, we took a break. I called Martha on the radio to ask her to send out

Sherlock with Holmes, his trackin' dog, so when we thought we'd got all the pieces, we could have 'em go over the place for any we might'a missed.

The next question was who was gonna pick up the "body." Ordinarily that's the coroner's job an' he delegates it to our local undertaker, who takes the deceased to his funeral parlor. Boone County ain't big enough to have its own morgue. In the rare case of murder, suicide, or death in suspicious circumstances, I ride in the hearse with the driver an' his cargo an' we detour to the state pathology lab, where they make do with a walk-in cooler. 'Cause there's a chain of custody to maintain, Doc Howard, who runs the place, puts a padlock on the door. In this case, I couldn't really see the undertaker gettin' involved.

Martha Rooney solved the dilemma for us. "Homer?" Her voice sounded farther away than usual over the radio.

"Yes, ma'am." I was restin' my rump against the trunk of a big old willow that leaned out over the river. Rye was balanced on a huge sideways branch that the state police boat was tied up underneath. Underhill was sittin' in the boat an' Yates straddlin' the big cooler he an' Underhill'd brought along. All us was listenin' for Martha's instructions.

"The coroner has just deputized you to take charge of the body," she told me. "You're to take it to the state medical lab for autopsy."

"Ain't no body."

"Well, take what you've got."

"Yes, ma'am. But ain't that a conflict of interest?"

"We all have every confidence you'll do the right thing."

The state troopers sniggered.

"Well, don't laugh yet, boys," I told 'em. "I'm hereby *offi*cially requestin' your assistance with pickin' up this here *ho*micide victim."

"You don't even know for sure these bones are human," Trooper Yates said.

"They're human."

"Oh, yeah?"

"I found a toe."

Underhill said, "I don't suppose it's got a printable surface attached?"

"That'd be contrary to the first law of criminal investigation."

"Which is?"

"Murphy's Law."

"Right. So it's doubtful you'll ever be able to identify this victim, let alone determine the cause of death."

"You may be right about identifyin' him, but the cause an' manner of death're clear."

Yates sneered. "In your crystal ball!"

I pointed out a skull fragment Rye an' I had located, one that had a neat hole through the middle, with the inside edges beveled toward the concave side. "Wanna bet?"

We'd just about got all the pieces of our victim bagged an' tagged when the Chicago detective showed. He'd hiked half a mile through God-knows-what in the way of swamp an' snake-infested thickets to get there from the road, an' he didn't waste any time on courtesies, just jumped right in. "I heard you found a body. Is it Devon?"

"Can't say yet," I told him, though I was thinkin' it'd be stretchin' things too far for it to be anybody else. An' anyway, there wasn't anyone else missin'. "But don't go gettin' all fired up 'til the pathologist's had a look-see. We ain't got enough of a body to be sure this weren't a dead bear."

Peter looked disappointed. I don't know why—he was

prob'ly gettin' paid by the day an' the most work he'd been doin' was channel surfin' back at the Motel Six.

I said, "This is a official crime scene. You'll have to clear out. If it turns out we found your man, we'll let you know."

"You just said it could be a bear."

"In that case, it'd be huntin' outta season. Which is also a crime."

Peter looked like a man who's just found hisself in the twilight zone. I had Rye escort him back to his car.

It was nearly dark by the time we was ready to have Holmes go over the scene. Thank God all he found was a bit of skull bone up in the crotch of a tree, where it fell when the crow that was nestin' there dropped it. We duly photographed an' diagrammed the tree, then sent Holmes home 'fore he could find anythin' else.

After we had all the bones an' bits packed in the cooler an' loaded in the boat, Trooper Yates got in the last word. "Deters," he said, "let me know next time you-all are fixin' to have a homicide in Boone County, so I can call in sick that day."

Child Welfare

It was nearly midnight by the time I delivered our victim to the state medical lab an' picked up my truck back in the swamp. I decided the paperwork'd keep 'til mornin'.

I didn't sleep real good. After eatin' breakfast at Denny's—on the interstate, where I wasn't knowed an' wouldn't be axed bout yesterday's goin's-on—I drove to the nearest One Hour Photo an' got my film developed. Then I headed back to West Wheeling to go to work.

Child Welfare, in the person of my sister, Penny Deters Evans, was waitin' in my office when I got there. Penny's a thin woman, near as tall as me, an' tougher'n a Marine. She said, "Homer, I got a crime to report."

I resisted the urge to tell her, Git in line. Instead, I said, "Yes, ma'am. What kin I do for you?"

She blinked. She's not used to me givin' her what she wants without a fight. "You can uphold the law." I waited. "Mavis Thistle is keeping her older girl out of school to baby-sit her younger ones."

"What'd you expect? You told her you was gonna take them kids away if she left 'em alone again."

"I expect her either to stay home with them herself or hire a competent adult to watch them."

Knowin' Mavis, I knew Penny was dreamin', but I didn't argue. "What do you want me to do about it?"

"You're the truant officer. Do your duty!"

I got out the truancy notice forms an' handed one to her. "Get this filled out by the kid's teacher an' bring it back."

After she left, I cataloged my developed film, an' put the date, roll number an' case number on all the negatives from each roll, then put the date, roll number, negative number, an' case number on the back of each pi'ture. The negatives went into labeled archive pages in a big notebook in the office safe, an' the prints—in sequence—went into labeled 8 1/2" x 11" album page sheets in the proper case files.

I had two of 'em. One was labeled ROGER DEVON. I decided it would be fittin' to call the other case PUZZLE MAN 'cause of the victim's condition. I figured I could add "WO" to the file label in front of MAN if *he* turned out to be a *she*. I had just started typin' a list from my field notes of what each photo was a pi'ture of, when Penny come back.

She slapped the form I'd given her down on my desk. "Here you are, Homer. Sic 'em!"

I looked it over. On it, the teacher stated that Dotty Thistle hadn't been to school in over a week, an' that her mother claimed she was sick. "This doesn't say nothin' about baby-sittin' young 'uns," I told Penny.

"Of course not. She told *me* she sent Dotty to stay with her sister, Eloise, in the city, where they have better schools."

"Well, you write out a statement that says that an' I'll have grounds to go out an' talk to her about it."

"Have you a form for that?"

"Not yet. This is the first time it's come up." I handed her a sheet of paper an' a pen. "Your lucky day. You get to make up your own form."

Penny went back to her office to make out her report, an' I put the truancy report in a file I called DOTTY THISTLE. Then I went back to my field notes. Penny was back long before I finished. I looked over her report an' put it in the Thistle file, on the corner of my desk.

She said, "Aren't you going to do something now?"

"Are these kids in imminent danger of physical harm?"

"No."

"Then I'll get to it soon's I got time."

"Homer!"

"I happen to be workin' on a death investigation here, which—like it or not—takes precedent over truancy." I folded my hands on the desk in front of me an' looked at her like I was waitin' for her to come up with some new, bigger problem.

I could see the wheels turnin' as she thought about it, an' I could almost see her decide she'd get my back up if she pushed it. She finally said, "Well, I appreciate your taking the time to talk with me, Deputy. I certainly hope you can fit us into your busy schedule sometime soon."

I decided to really throw her for a loop. I just said, "Yes, ma'am."

I finished typin' up my reports an' filed 'em just about lunchtime. I hadn't et in town for nearly a week an' I hadn't seen Nina for two days, so I decided to stop by the post office an' feel her out about goin' to lunch with me. I called Martha to tell her I'd be ten-seven, an' headed across the street.

Nina was wearin' a dress that fit like it was painted on. She was standin' behind the counter, so I couldn't see her legs, but the rest of her looked fine. There weren't no bumps or ridges I could see to show she was wearin' nothin' under the dress. The lump I suddenly felt in my throat was as big as a man's heart. I swallowed. I took off my hat an' held it by the brim, in front of my fly. Just to distract Nina—in case she was noticin' the stir her outfit was causin'—I nodded at the stack of Wanted posters. She'd used an orange marker to draw bull's-eyes over the faces, along with enough circles around the bull's-eyes to make each poster into a dandy target. The felon of the day was Ransom Thomas, bank robber, strong-arm bandit, an' escape artist.

"Looks like what they say about the devil is true," I told her, noddin' at the posters.

"Which particular *say* is that?"

" 'Bout him findin' work for idle minds—'pears you don't have enough real work to keep you busy."

She got all uptight, like a woman whose new dress ain't been noticed, an' sniffed. "Show's what you know. If you don't do somethin' to spice up them posters, no one even notices 'em. Might as well have pi'tures of Rocky an' Bullwinkle. As I see it, I'm doin' the Law a favor."

I had to admit she was right, but I didn't. I said, "You wanna go to lunch?"

"Not a chance!"

As I shook my head an' turned to leave, I did manage to get the last word in: "Nice dress."

the ME's report

When I called Martha after lunch to tell her I was ten-eight, she told me to call Doc Howard. I did. *He* told me to come pick up my jigsaw puzzle.

"Ain't you gonna do a autopsy?"

"What's to autopsy? You come get your box of parts so I can have my cooler back."

The pathology lab at the state medical school always gives me the creeps. The big walk-in cooler has dead bodies laid out in it like turkeys in the meat section at Saveway. Doc Howard ain't at all bothered—he's been doin' this since Moby Dick was a minnow. When I got there, he went in the cooler an' come out with the state cops' ice chest. It had a manila envelope duct-taped to the lid with the chain of custody form stuck to the outside with sticky tape. Half a dozen signatures'd been added to the form since I'd seen it last.

"You been passin' my victim around like the latest joke," I complained.

"I had faculty members from several specialties look at him. Their reports are in the envelope as addenda to mine."

"So you figured out he was male. What else?"

"Yes. We were able to reconstruct enough of the pelvic girdle to determine sex, and the beveling around the hole in his frontal bone fragment makes the cause and manner of death rather apparent."

I held up my hands. "Just gimme the short version, Doc. In English."

He sighed like talkin' to me was a pitiful waste of his time. "The bottom line is that all we can tell you is that your victim, a male who was probably in good antemortem health, was shot through the skull before or very shortly after death. He was subsequently consumed—eaten in the vernacular—by large carnivores, probably bears." He gave me a Happy-now? look an' waited.

"Thanks, Doc. That pretty much confirms what we figured. Any idea how old he was or how long he's been dead?"

"He was old enough for the cranial sutures to have closed and the long-bone ends to have ossified, but not old enough to have any osteoporosis or arthritis—at least not in the joints you've got there. My guess is he was between eighteen and thirty-five. As for time of death, the condition of the remaining cartilage and ligament is consistent with a period between a few days and a couple of months."

"Anythin' else I should know?"

"Nothing comes to mind."

"One more thing—Was he shot from the front or the back?"

"If the bullet had impacted just an inch lower, it would have hit him between the eyes."

the Thistle place

I figured I'd better stop at the Thistle place on my way back to the office. It was a two-story, once-white frame house with a gable roof, a peelin' green door an' shutters, an' a screen porch across the front. All the windows had dingy curtains, all shut. The screen door sagged open, an' the front steps was broke. The condition of the house kinda reminded me of the Jackson place, but at least Ash kept his yard decent. Thistles' drive was a collection of potholes hangin' together outta habit, an' the yard was overgrowed with weeds an' overflowed with junk, from empty food cans to dead white goods. The whole place looked just like what'd happened—the man run off an' left the wife with a run-down house an' too many kids to handle. Mavis Thistle had give up on livin' an' was drinkin' herself to death—along with all that come with drinkin'.

I kept a eye on the front as I shut off the car an' got out. If I hadn't been watchin' for it, I would'a missed the little movement from the curtain in one of the windows near the door. Mavis didn't have a dog—even with the checks from Child Welfare she could hardly feed her kids. An' nobody with two bits to his name'd board with her an' those outta-control kids. So unless it was Mavis herself behind that curtain, Penny was likely right about Dotty bein' home baby-sittin'.

I rang the bell but didn't hear it ring inside, so I knocked.

Nothin' happened. I knocked again, louder. After a third knock, a muffled voice—sounded female—said, "Who's there?"

"Deputy Sheriff Deters."

"Whatcha want?"

"I wanna talk to you."

"You got a warrant?"

"Nope."

"Go away."

"Be easier on you if you don't make me get a warrant."

This time she didn't answer. I knocked again, but didn't get nothin' more. After a few more minutes of starin' at the ratty door, I went back to my car an' drove off.

search warrants

The search warrant contained words like "Squalor an' Filth," words the judge'd have to look up in his Thorndike an' Barnhart dictionary. Time I got done, I was on a roll. I felt so good I wrote up another warrant just for the hell of it—to search Ash Jackson's place.

Out here in the country, the circuit court judges really do ride a circuit—there ain't enough business to keep 'em busy in any one town. Tuesday was West Wheeling's court day, an' it wasn't Tuesday, so I had to go all the way to Okra to get my search warrants issued. Me bein' from outta town, the Okrans let me go ahead of 'em. Or maybe they was just curious as to what kind of crimes afflict our town. Anyway, the judge looked over my paperwork an' signed the warrant to search the Thistle place without comment. Then he held up the other one an' axed, "What's your probable, Homer?"

I pointed to the paper. "Like it says there, Judge. We got some human remains unaccounted for, an' a missin' man—mebbe the same man as the remains. An' Ash Jackson was the last one seen with him."

"Says here you got a reliable informant. Who?"

I stepped up to the bench so no one but the judge could hear me ax, "Off the record?" The judge didn't say no, so I said, "Rye Willis."

"Rye? He's a moonshiner."

"You drink his shine?"

"Doesn't everyone?"

"I rest my case."

"Humph. Says here you hope to find evidence of a murder: blood, personal property of the victim—that should be *the alleged victim*—guns and drugs. 'Course you're gonna find guns and drugs. Everybody knows Ash's got more guns than the national armory, and everybody in Boone County has—"

"Okay. Okay," I said. "How 'bout if I change it to *illegal* guns an' drugs?"

"That wording would be acceptable."

I wondered where he learnt a word like "acceptable."

Ash's place revisited

Ash's place looked like the ATF'd been through it. The door'd been kicked open, the jamb splintered. I was careful goin' through it. Inside, the front room'd been tossed an' scrambled. Any place you could think to hide anythin' was open an' emptied or smashed an' dumped out on the floor. Even the stereo an' CD player was in pieces. Ash's furniture was early American, an' he had a couple nice antiques. They were all up-ended; most were broken. His papers was in a pile with the desk turned upside down on top. The braided rug'd been heaped at one end of the room. Enough of the pine floorboards'd been pried loose to make a hole a man could put his head through. I made a mental note to look into it as soon as I was sure there was nothin' in the house would jump on me if I got down on all fours.

I went on to look in the kitchen an' found the same general situation. Everything'd been opened an' dumped out, from cabinets to tin cans. Somebody with more guts than brains'd even taken a ax to the aerosol cans, someone who'd read—in one of those Build-Yourself-a-Arsenal magazines—'bout cans with hidden compartments. I stayed outta there to avoid trackin' the flour an' smashed eggs around.

The bathroom an' bedroom were the same. Stuff dumped out in the sink an' tub, in the toilet, an' on the floor. The closets'd been emptied, the light fixtures broke, pi'tures took off the walls, even the wall outlet covers were off. A kitchen chair'd been dragged up under the open trap door to the attic space. I was real cautious puttin' my head up there, but I needn't a been. Somethin' *had* been up there—all the ceiling insulation was tore up. But that was all I saw—that an' dust motes dancin' in the sunbeams sneakin' through the attic vent louver.

I went back out the front, an' made a quick tour of the yard. I didn't see no one so I guessed it was safe to go back in an' stick my head in the crawl space. There was nothin' there but pea gravel an' spider webs. I come up for air an' went outside for a think.

Ash's front porch view was finer than he deserved. I sat on the weathered steps an' admired it. The sky was bluer than Nina's eyes an' dotted with ripe-cotton clouds. The air smelled a little like cut grass an' old compost. An old burr oak tree held the line between the grass an' woods, an' a pair of little birds chased a big old crow from outta the tree clear outta the yard. A red-winged blackbird was singin'. The grass was a week's worth taller'n last time I seen it, but it was summer sweet an' shimmerin' in the breeze like ripples on a green lake. There was some dandelions still bloomin' like bright splashes of yellow paint on the grass, but most were blown an' gone. The bright sunlight made the shadows on the porch an' under the trees look black an' mysterious.

I tried to guess why Ash'd leave all this—even supposin' he'd killed the missionary. It'd been more in his nature to brass it out, not run 'til the warrant was served. His boat was gone, an' his fishin' gear. There wasn't a gun or a cartridge in sight. If he'd cleared out for good, it made sense that he'd take those. But why leave everythin' else? Why not sell it, or give it to his kin? An' who smashed the place? An' when? An' why? An' what the hell was I supposed to do about it? I must've gone over it for fifteen minutes without thinkin' of anythin' useful.

Eventually I did the right thing. I got out my camera an' took pi'tures. Then I dusted damn near everything with fingerprint powder. I got maybe half a dozen prints. After photographin' 'em in place, I lifted 'em with tape an' saved 'em on cards, each labeled an' dated. 'Fore I went back to the office to write my report, I dropped the fingerprint cards off at the state cop shop so they could run 'em through their computer. Then I stopped at Rooney's to report in person. Ben listened to the whole story without comment. Martha give me tea an' sympathy.

the Boone dispute

If you counted Ash Jackson, I now had two missin' persons an' a dead body—parts, anyway. Ash was probably AWOL voluntary 'cause someone was after him, but it was a real coincidence—all that happenin' at once. Law enforcement tends to disbelieve in coincidences. However, I still didn't have enough of a good idea what was goin' on to work it all out. So I decided to fall back on that old law enforcement standby—procedure. If I kept followin' through on all my leads, an' made thorough reports of everythin', sooner or later I'd have enough pieces to make a pi'ture. That was my theory, anyhow. As for the truancy matter, it was pretty late by the time I got my pi'tures of Ash's place developed, an' since the Thistle warrant was good 'til the next day noon, I guessed I'd wait 'til tomorrow mornin'. Then I could take Penny when I went out to the Thistle place.

As soon as I wrote up the report on the break-in, I needed to talk to Angie Boone. In fact, as murder investigations go, this one was pretty lame without me havin' talked to one of the chief—maybe—witnesses.

Interviewin' her was gonna be a tricky proposition 'cause Angie was at that awkward age where she could run off an' marry someone without her folks' permission, but if she stuck around, her folks could claim she was a minor an' refuse to let me talk to her. I also needed to conduct my interview in town—somewhere I could deputize Penny or Nina or Alethia to search her if I had to actually take her into custody. I thought about the problem all the way back to town.

I thought about it off an' on while I did the paperwork on the break-in. I was still thinkin' about it when Len Hartman shouted, "Sheriff! Trouble. Post office! Come quick!" He was jumpin' up an' down under my office window—the one that faces Cross Street—like he'd stepped on a fire ants' nest.

When I got there, all hell had broke loose. Mars Boone was standin' in front of the counter shakin' a paper bag in the direction of his daughter, Angie, who was standin' behind Nina. Nina was behind the counter with her twelve-gauge aimed at Mars. Angie was wailin' like a banshee, wringin' her hands like some soap opera character. Mars was yellin' at his wife, who was standin' next to him, yellin' right back.

Mrs. Boone spotted me an' screeched, "Sheriff, thank God you're here."

Everybody shut up an' looked at me like I was some kind of Mr. Fix-it. I figured it'd be safest to play along an' said, "Nina, put that gun away. Mars, back off. Somebody tell me what's goin' on!"

They all started talkin' at once. I bellowed, "Shut up, all a you!" It was an old Sheriff Rooney trick, actin' madder or crazier'n anyone else. It worked. They all got quiet an' waited for further orders. "That's better," I said, reasonably. "Now, s'posin'—startin' with Nina—you tell me what's goin' on."

Nina put her twelve-gauge away. "Damned if I know, Homer. Angie run in here screamin' he was gonna kill her, so I got out my gun. Then Mars run in here yellin' he was gonna kill her. Then Miz Boone run in here shoutin' at Mars not to kill her. Then Len run outta here like the devil was after him, hollerin' he was gonna call the Law. Then you showed up." She shrugged.

I said, "Mars?"

Mars was red as a preacher caught with his pants down in a whorehouse. He shoved the paper bag at me an' shook it, then shook it at his oldest girl. "I caught that little slut with this—This—" He couldn't bring hisself to say what. He shoved the paper bag in my direction.

I took it an' looked inside.

"There ain't but one reason she'd have one of those—" He still couldn't say it.

I said, "Angie, what you got to say for yourself?"

"It ain't none of your business, Homer. Or his, either." She nodded at her pa. "I'm old enough, I don't have to account to him no more." She looked like she was scared shitless, but she clenched her fists an' shoved her jaw out.

"You sixteen?" I axed.

She nodded.

Mars looked like he'd been pole-axed. Whatever he'd been plannin' to happen, I guess that wasn't it. "Have it your way," he said, quietly, like he was too mad to trust hisself to talk. "But I don't ever want to see your face again." He turned to Mrs. Boone an' said, "Come on, wife," an' stalked out. Myra Boone looked like she'd been slapped. She gave Angie as sorrowful a look as I ever seen, then turned without a word an' followed Mars. Angie started gnawin' on her thumb knuckle.

The post office was quiet as a graveyard for a good long minute before Nina said, "For God's sake, Homer, what's in that bag?"

I didn't feel much like sayin' in front of ladies, so I handed her the bag. She didn't have any such reservations. She took one look an' turned around to Angie an' said, "Girl, are you pregnant?!"

What was in the bag was a home pregnancy test.

Angie said, "None of your business, either, Miz Ross."

Nina did what she always does durin' family emergencies—closed the post office. Then she dragged Angie in the back room an' sat her down at the table she's got there. Nobody told me not to, so I tagged along.

After half a hour of tellin' us it was none of our business, Angie broke down an' admitted she was for-a-fact pregnant, but claimed she didn't know by who. Finally, an' with a straight face, she said a angel had come to her in a dream an' knocked her up. She held fast to this particular story until we gave up tryin' to get her to change it. I *did* ask, at one point, if the angel's name was Ash Jackson; she got huffy an' said, "Gross! No way!"

"You got any idea what you're gonna do, girl?" Nina axed. "Where you're gonna go? How you're gonna live?"

"I'll think of somethin'."

"Yeah. Well, while you're thinkin', you best stay with me." Nina waited to see if that was all right.

Angie nodded cautiously.

"An' you can earn your keep by helpin' out around here."

Angie nodded again.

"The baby's father, he likely to—?"

"Ain't got no father! It was a angel."

Nina said, "Horsefeathers!"

An' I wondered if the angel was Roger Devon.

Angie Boone

I hung around the post office, waitin' for a chance to get Angie Boone alone, 'til Nina threw me out, then I went back to the town hall to arrange with Penny to have *her* serve the Thistle warrant. I headed back across the street about closin' time. Nina was takin' care of all the folks who'd waited 'til five-to-five to get their business done—maybe eight of 'em, two with packages. I busied myself lookin' at the Wanted posters. The felon of the day was Leon Whistlesmith, car thief an' burglar.

"Homer," Nina said, "you got business here or you jus' holdin' up the line?"

"I got to ask Angie somethin'. She still here?"

"Where else'd she be?"

"Gone home, maybe?"

"She's in the back. Now, get outta the way."

I managed not to grin as I went past.

Angie was sittin' cross-legged on the cot Nina keeps in the back for naps an' the few days when she gets snowed in in town. Along with the cot, there's a table an' three straight-back chairs, an' a poster with a poem called *Desiderata.* Angie was readin' a paperback romance, which she put down when I come in. She looked at the door behind me—must've been hopin' Nina would come to her rescue. I grabbed one of the chairs an' turned it around so I could straddle it, an' crossed my arms on the back—a little strategy I learned for questionin' skitterish witnesses. Puttin' the chair between you's supposed to make you seem less threatenin'.

Angie did one of those acts—which I'm sure she got from watchin' TV—where she looked from side to side, like she was tryin' to find who else I might be starin' at. When I didn't say nothin', she put the book down an' said, *"What?"*

"What do you know about Roger Devon?"

Whatever she was expectin', that weren't it. She put her hands together over her belly like she'd been punched. Then she pulled herself together an' said, "Nothin'."

"You an' I both know that ain't true."

Her mouth got all hard an' she tried to stare me down. But I've had more experience with face-offs. She said, "He was one of my teachers. He quit."

"Why?" I said, though I had a good idea it was related to the state she was in.

She shrugged. I waited. She outwaited me.

"Where'd he go?"

"How would I know?" I waited. "Back to Illinois?"

"How'd you know he was from there?"

"Must'a heard talk. What's this about?"

"Devon's missin'. An' I got a unidentified body on my hands might be him. You know anythin' about that?"

She shuddered. "No, an' I don't wanna."

"I got it on good authority Devon was a friend a yours."

"Who tole you that?"

"I can't reveal my sources."

"Gossip!"

"Well?"

"He was nice."

"You an' him kinda left the mission together."

That got to her. "No!" She realized how much she was

givin' herself away, 'cause I could see her make a effort to relax. Then she said, "I was thinking of quitting anyway. An' the sub they got us was real bad, so I quit."

"Uh-hunh."

"I don't care if you don't believe me!"

"I didn't say I don't believe you."

She got a pouty look on her face an' picked up her book, held it like she couldn't wait for me to leave an' let her get back to it.

"Why'd Devon leave?"

"I don't know." I waited. "I heard Ash Jackson run him off."

"Where'd you hear?"

"Around."

"What else you hear?"

"Nothin'."

"I think you know more."

"I don't know nothin' an' I don't want to hear no more. I don't want to talk to you."

"You have to. I'm the Law."

"Leave me alone!"

Just then, the door opened an' Nina swarmed in. She pretty much got the lay of the land at a glance, 'cause she said, "Homer, get the hell out!"

I got up faster'n I'd set down an' put the chair between us.

"An' tell Mars Boone he's lower'n a rattler's belly!" Nina added.

"What's Mars got to do with anythin'?"

second body—no teeth

The crows was the giveaway. I could see 'em hangin' up in the dead tops of the willows linin' the drainage ditch long before I spotted Mars Boone's truck. They was waitin' for Mars to clear out an' let 'em go back to feedin'. Mars's truck was alongside the ditch, an' he was standin' with his back to it. He looked a bit green, under his farmer's tan, 'bout ready to pass out. He pointed past hisself, to what was interestin' the crows. I got out to take a look.

Personally, dead bodies don't bother me 'less it's someone I know. This one, I couldn't tell if I knew—somebody'd blowed his head off. Someone didn't want us to ID the body. I looked long enough to get a *i*dea of what'd happened. Someone'd dumped the body—or maybe brought it live—into the ditch, then blowed off the lower half of its face with a shotgun. Then he—or she, let's not be sexist—covered up the remains with a old blanket an' a piece of cardboard, prob'ly to keep the crows from findin' it 'fore the maggots done their work. The killer hadn't figured on coyotes, or dogs—whatever—something'd dragged the blanket off to get at the free lunch underneath. The coverings looked pretty much like what some folks carry in their trunks, an' that pretty much let Mars off the hook. Like most farmers, he carries a shovel to bury roadkill. If he'd done it, he'd have buried the evidence.

I returned to where he was waitin' with his back to the

scene. If the shovel argument wasn't enough to clear him, his puke-green color would've. I got my hip flask outta the squad an' shoved it at him.

"Here, Mars."

"I don't drink."

"This is medicinal. Don't want you passin' out 'fore I get a statement."

He took the flask an' had a swig. I watched his eyes bug as it went down. He wheezed, but his face went a shade closer to livin' color.

"Lemme use your phone," I said.

He didn't even ask why, when I had a radio—just give it to me. I called Martha, to give her the news, then the state boys. Sergeant Underhill answered.

"This is Deputy Sheriff Deters," I said. "I'm afraid I got another body."

"This is getting to be a trend, isn't it, Deputy?"

"It ain't really local. An' I got no control over interstate commerce."

"Which isn't local, victim or perp?"

"Neither, I'd say. Looks like yet another case of fly dumpin'."

"Not toxic, just wasted?"

I groaned. He axed for directions an' said he'd be along directly.

While we waited, I got a statement from Mars. He confirmed what I suspected. He'd been out drivin' around his farm, mindin' his own business, when he spotted the crows. An' he'd stopped an' got his shovel out, plannin' to deprive the varmints of their road pizza.

Even though it smelled God-awful an' was crawlin' with maggots, our second victim didn't take half as long to collect—not as many pieces. The state cops helped me get it in a body bag an' lift that into the borrowed hearse.

Usually I don't go to autopsies, but for this guy I figured I could make a exception. One of Doc's grad students helped me unload. Doc was already gowned an' gloved, an' ready to go when we got to the lab.

"You tryin' to set a speed record for autopsies, Doc?" I axed him.

"You trying to set some kind of record for number of homicides in Boone County, Homer?"

"I axed first."

"We're having a graduation open house here in a couple of weeks. I don't want the place smelling of overripe carrion. That odor is very difficult to get out."

"Yeah."

Just 'cause Doc is fast, don't mean he wasn't thorough. He took samples of the critters, which he sent off to the entomology lab with one of the students who looked ready to pass out. I took pi'tures of the remains, front an' back, fore Doc an' the two remainin' kids undressed the body. Doc had one of 'em hang up the clothes to dry while he went over the corpse for any trace evidence—hairs, fibers, gravel, excetera—he could find. It all went into little numbered paper envelopes for the state crime lab, an' Doc noted every sample an' specimen on his tape recorder. When he was pretty well satisfied he'd got everythin' there was to find, they washed the rest of the wildlife down the sink an' cleaned up the victim. I took more pi'tures, an' Doc took a bunch of X-rays before openin' up.

He started off with his standard line: "I have before me the body of a well developed, well nourished, white male who appears to be between forty and sixty years of age . . ."

That left Roger Devon out.

"Can't you narrow it down a decade or so, Doc?"

"Sorry. It depends on how well he took care of himself. Since we don't know, I can't say. I *can* tell you, that apart from the face and hands, there isn't too much damage that was caused by the killer. But there's your cause of death." He pointed to a couple of stab wounds in the victim's neck and throat. "He bled to death. The killer probably just used the shotgun to obliterate his identity."

"Yeah," I said. "It looked to me like he was killed somewhere else an' dumped."

"Very likely." He poked around what was left of the head. "I can't be positive, because there's so much missing, but my guess is, this guy didn't have any teeth."

"That'd explain why we couldn't find 'em."

The rest of the autopsy was pretty standard. I had to hang around to the end, 'cause I had to take the body back with me—Doc insisted. The victim's clothes were dry by the time we had their owner back in the hearse. We sorted all the little envelopes by type of evidence, an' started a chain of custody sheet for the hair an' fibers, another for trace evidence, an' one for shotgun pellets, excetera. Doc signed for the tissue samples he was keepin'—for further study—an' we sent forms up to the entomology department for the maggots. I took charge of the film, promisin' to send Doc a set of prints.

By the time I dropped off the clothes an' envelopes at the state crime lab, dropped the body—"Headless" as I was beginnin' to call him—at the funeral parlor, an' got the film developed, it was supper time. It occurred to me I hadn't had lunch, but I took the pi'tures back to my office an' locked them in the safe before headin' for the Truck Stop.

I had to pass the Boones's farm on the way to supper. It was botherin' me so much that the perpetrator had got away with hidin' Headless's identity, that I turned off an' went back to the crime scene. I got out my road-kill shovel an' started diggin' through the dirt in the ditch where the body'd been. I was hopin' we'd missed somethin' that would identify Headless. We hadn't. So I walked around the spot in a widenin' spiral. It was my lucky day or mebbe the angle of the sun was just right. 'Bout sixteen feet from where Mars found the body, right where it must've been blowed by the shotgun blast, I spotted a pinkie finger. It was curled an' dried like a hunk of old beef jerky, but I didn't care. It *had* to belong to Headless—his was the only body out here missin' parts. An' I was happy as a possum in a pantry to have somethin' with a fingerprint on it. I planted my shovel where its shadow'd mark the spot, an' went back for my camera.

the KKK

The next day was Saturday. I'd made kind of a late night of it, celebratin' my big find the previous evenin', so I wasn't feelin' my best. Still, I'd just about finished writin' up all the reports on Headless, when Nina called me to report "trespassin' an' vandalism" at the post office. Normally all that would constitute a major crime wave in West Wheeling, an' I'd rush over to investigate, but with all that'd gone down in the last week, I wasn't real enthusiastic. I finished my report an' locked the files an' photos in the safe 'fore I left the office.

I found Nina standin' on the porch with her hands on her hips, starin' daggers at a poster stapled to the post office wall. It was one of those things you can have made up from your own negative, an' showed Rufus "Ruthless" Groggins an' four of his henchmen standin' in a line, showin' off their artillery: M16s, sawed-off shotguns, even a Molotov cocktail. The writin' at the top said "KKK," an' underneath the pi'ture it said, "THE FEW, THE PROUD, THE READY."

Contrary to popular belief, most of the black folks in Boone County work three times as hard for half the pay as most whites, so I try to cut 'em some slack in my dealin's with 'em. An' I do what I can to keep a lid on the Klan. Ruthless heads up our local chapter, though it ain't any great shakes. Years back, shortly after Ben Rooney become sheriff, Ruthless tried to head up a big rally. He called on the local press an' put flyers up all over town, but he didn't reckon on my ma, who—at the time—was town librarian. She axed everybody who come in for a book, "What if the Klan held a rally and nobody came?" All three of the local ministers picked up on that an' told their congregations to stay away, an' the sheriff pretty much suggested to everybody who drifted into town to gawk, that they might find some fine bargains over at the Wal-Mart. Then he called up the Wal-Mart manager an' dropped the hint that Klan Rally Day'd be a fine day for a sale—even promised to advertise it free.

I missed the show 'cause Sheriff Rooney sent me to work crowd control at the west end of town an' *di*vert everybody to the big sale. The sheriff deputized my ma an' Nina's to do the same at the east end, so they pretty much missed the action, too. However, the long an' the short of it was nobody showed up at the rally but the Klan, an' the sheriff, an' Abner Davis, our only local reporter. What he reported was a major traffic jam at Wal-Mart. Still, Ruthless never gives up.

Nina pointed at the poster. "Can't you do somethin' about that, Homer? They're really givin' our friendly town a bad name."

"I don't know, Nina. Not unless one of them weapons is illegal to possess. Their right to assemble an' run off at the mouth is protected by the First Amendment."

Nina studied the poster. "Would you say a Molotov cocktail is a *de*structive *de*vice?"

"I guess it wouldn't be much of a stretch."

"Then go get that ATF feller that's been snoopin' around an' tell him we got some business for him."

"What're you talkin' about?"

She said, "Come here once." She ducked inside the post office an' reached a red paperback book out from under the counter—*ARSON: The Complete Investigator's Manual.* She opened it an' stabbed page six with her pointin' finger. "It says here, *Title II requires that various 'destructive devices' be registered with the ATF in order to be legally possessed. . . .*" She hitched her thumb at the *o*ffendin' poster on the porch. "Wanna bet that there's registered?"

"Not really. Anyway, they'd just say it was fake, an' how'd you prove it wasn't?"

"Get a search warrant an' *eggs*amine it."

"You must think I got nothin' better to do."

"I *know* you got nothin' better to do, Homer."

"Yeah, right. I got two unsolved homicides an' truants runnin' rampant, I ain't located our missin' missionary yet, but I got time to harass the Klan?"

"Maybe if you'd go talk to Ruthless, you'll find he's mixed up in them other things."

"The Klan didn't kill our Boone farm victim—he weren't black or Jewish."

"How'd you know he weren't Jewish?"

"I was at the autopsy."

She didn't get it 'til I gave her a just-think-about-it look. Then she did an' blushed. Finally she said, "There ain't nothin' more you can do about all them other things, so you may as well do somethin' about Ruthless."

Her mind was made up; there was no confusin' her with facts. I decided to hit her up with one of her own tactics—misdirection. "Where'd you get that book?"

"It come in the mail."

"Yeah? Addressed to who?" It was the same book I'd ordered an' sent $19.50 for, includin' shippin' an' handlin'. I hadn't got my book yet, an' it was too much of a coincidence to believe Nina'd somehow thought to order the same one.

"Well, all right. It's yours. The package was ripped an' I ain't got round to repackin' it yet."

I thought I had her. "Ain't there some regulation 'gainst postal employees readin' people's mail?"

But she just handed me her postal regulations book an' said, "You're welcome to look."

Motel Six

I prob'ly never would've missed ATF agent Arnold if Nina hadn't been so keen on me turnin' in the Klan. The folks at Motel Six hadn't seen him lately, though he hadn't checked out. I sweet-talked Lucy, the housekeeper, into lettin' me have a look 'round his room. It 'peared like he'd unpacked half his stuff an' shaved 'fore leavin'. Lucy said he hadn't touched nothin' in three days.

There wasn't a whole lot else to do after that but wait. If I called ATF to ask what was up, they'd deny sendin' a agent or tell me to mind my own damn business. An' if he was really missin', they'd send another couple of turkeys—who wouldn't be the least use in findin' Arnold—to complicate my life. I decided to put him at the bottom of my folks-to-find list an' wait 'til I had evidence of foul play 'fore makin' a federal case of it.

'Fore I left the motel, I looked up our visitin' detective. When he opened his door an' spotted me, he looked hopeful as a convict who's just had his sentence reduced to time served. "You find him?" he axed. He kept standin' in the doorway blockin' my view of the room 'til I wondered if he had a woman in there, or drugs.

I said, " 'Fraid not."

"But you just found another body. The whole town's talkin' about it."

"Mind if I come in?"

Peter took a quick look behind him—no doubt checkin' to be sure there was nothin' in the room I shouldn't see. As he stepped away from the door, he grabbed the coat off the chair next to it an' tossed it on the dresser. It neatly covered the police scanner he had set up there, but not 'fore I spotted it. I didn't let on I seen it, though it explained how Peter'd managed to show up in the swamp when he did.

He pointed at the empty chair. "Have a seat and tell me about this latest body." He sat hisself down on the end of the bed.

The room looked pretty lived in. The motel'd kept up housekeepin', but that didn't extend to hangin' up clothes or unpackin'. Peter's stuff lay 'round on every flat surface an' overflowed his suitcases. An' the table was covered with half-full bottles of booze an' mixers, an' half-empty bags of chips an' pretzels. I'd a bet fifty bucks the bathroom was a mess, too, in spite of Lucy.

"Don't get your hopes up. It were a older fella. Probably some guy ran afoul of the mob in the city, an' got hisself whacked."

"You didn't come all the way out here to tell me you *didn't* find Roger Devon."

"Well, I was hopin' you might could help me out with somethin' else."

He stood up. "Cut the corn-pone, deputy. I've been asking around about you and I'm not going to fall for your country Columbo routine."

I stood, too. "Well, if you wanna put it like that, Mr. Peter, I'm conductin' a *in*vestigation into two deaths an' a couple suspicious disappearances, an' I expect you to cooperate."

"I've already told you why I'm here, Deters. So far I've been stonewalled, cheated, and *continued*. I'd like nothing better than to finish my job and shake the dust of this place."

I'd heard about the "cheated" the previous evenin', when I was out celebratin'. I said, "If you're cryin' foul 'cause you severely underestimated our local pool sharks, you oughtta be ashamed. You're old enough to know better'n to try hustlin' hustlers on their home turf.

"As for the other stuff, I been busy an' ain't heard. How is it you been *stonewalled and postponed?*"

"I haven't gotten a single hard fact from you or anyone else since I got here. And that shyster that passes for a judge, told me he was giving me a continuance so he could *'consider the merits of my petition.'* For a court order to get a forwarding address, for Christ's sake!"

I shrugged, then hitched my thumb in the general direction of Arnold's room. "Not to change the subject much, but you seen the guy in 108 lately?"

"I've never seen him. Who is he? And what's your interest?"

"Claims he's with ATF. I got no interest in him, but I *do* have business with him."

"What does he look like?"

a "borrowed" poster

Nina was just closin' the post office for the weekend when I got back to town. She didn't even wait 'til I got my car parked 'fore she was yellin' for me to "come quick." I took my time. Quick is not the way I prefer to come.

"What is it you're so all-fired fired-up about now?" I axed her when I finally got parked an' crossed the street.

"One of my Wanted posters is missin'."

"Good Lord, girl. I got three missin' persons, two murders, an' truancy runnin' rampant, an' you want me to investigate a missin' poster?"

"Well, who'd you s'pose'd take a Wanted poster?"

"Probably someone who wanted a target an' is too cheap to buy one."

"Nobody's that hard up. Not to take a chance on *me* catchin' him. It had to be someone didn't want us to recognize the guy in the pi'ture."

"Who?"

"How do I know?"

"Who was it a poster of?"

"I can't remember."

"Well, if you don't even know whose pi'ture it was, how'm I s'posed to go after him."

"I don't know, Homer. You're the sheriff. I thought you'd have some ideas."

"Tell you what. You 'member his name, I'll have the state cops fax me a pi'ture."

heavy trafficking

I ain't one for goin' to church, except for weddin's an' funerals, though I do put on a clean uniform the Sundays I work. This Sunday I was workin' an' I had all the open case files out on my desk. I was tryin' to set up one of those charts where you put all the names across the top, other pertinent information down the side, an' X in the places where a pertinent fact applies to a particular name. I put a *X* in all the places where I could be fairly sure a fact—like missin' or dead—applied to the party in question, a *O* where I could be pretty certain that a fact couldn't apply—like Arnold bein' the father of Angie Boone's kid—an' a *?* if the fact might apply, however unlikely it was.

What I ended up with was:

	Devon	Ash	Arnold	Puzzle Man	Headless
missing	X	X	X	O	O
dead	?	?	?	X	X
killer 1	?	?	O	O	?
killer 2	O	?	?	O	O
father of AB's kid	?	?	O	?	?

After playin' with the possibilities for a time, I added Angie an' Peter to the top line, an' *O*s an' *?*s to show neither of 'em was dead or missin'; Angie might have killed either victim but didn't father her own child; an' Peter might'a killed Headless, but not Puzzle Man, an' he almost certainly wasn't the father of Angie's unborn kid. My chart looked like a scratch game of tic-tac-toe, but I couldn't think of nothin' else to do just then 'cept say to myself, Cheer up, Homer, things could be worse. I should'a knocked wood.

My thinkin' was interrupted, suddenly, by horns honkin' an' brakes squealin' outside on Main Street. This is highly *un*usual for Sunday mornin', when most of our citizens are either in church or home sleepin' off Saturday night. Of course, I got up an' had a look. Main Street seemed like the city in rush hour—cars an' trucks bumper to bumper in both directions. Lot of 'em were blowin' the four-way stop at Cross an' peelin' off down that street as well. There was more *ve*hicles in sight than I'd've bet were even registered in Boone County. A lot of 'em had outta state plates.

I grabbed the phone an' dialed the state *po*lice. "This is Deputy Sheriff Deters, West Wheeling," I tole the dispatcher. "What in hell's goin' on?"

She tole me. A waste-oil tanker'd turned over on the interstate, westbound, an' blocked the westbound lanes. An' the sludge it was carryin' had run down onto the eastbound lanes an' put them out of commission, too. "It's a mess," she said. "I hope you don't have another murder you need help with, Deputy, 'cause we got every man, woman, and draftee out there with the EPA trying to clean it up."

"I don't s'pose you got any detours marked?"

"I guess not if you're callin' about it."

"Thanks a bunch," I said, an' hung up. I got out my crowd control bullhorn, my traffic citation book, an' a pile of accident report forms. I figured I'd need 'em.

I went downstairs an' was about to go out the door when

the Evangelical Congregational Church service let out—or maybe they broke early 'cause of the commotion outside. Anyway, Nina was at the head of the pack that come filin' outta the town hall council room. When I spotted her, I had to take a step back, an' I nearly fell over the congregation's portable notice board.

It was the first time I ever saw all of her in a dress. It came to just below her knees, an' the sight made *my* knees a little wobbly. Her legs were just as pretty as I'd imagined. The rest of her looked fine, too. I took off my hat without thinkin', an' stood there, starin' in awe.

Nina pretended not to take much notice. She was studyin' the notice board message: THE LARGEST ROOM IN THE WORLD IS THE ROOM FOR IMPROVEMENT, though I'm sure she knew it by heart.

I might've stood there all mornin' 'cept just then there was the screech of metal scrapin' metal, lots more honkin', an' some major takin' of the Lord's name in vain.

That got to the congregation, which was pilin' up behind Nina. I led the parade outside, where we discovered a semi-truck'd overturned on top of several cars. Weren't no *people* hurt, but the truck'd split open, liberatin' its cargo: what seemed like thousands of white chickens was escapin' in every direction. At least half a dozen cars, that I could see, had run into the back of the truck in a huge chain reaction, an' a couple had run off the street to avoid a tail-ender. Motorists trapped by the wreckage were streamin' outta their cars. Chaos was buildin'. The situation called for organization, an' I was suddenly glad for my stint in the army. When in doubt, get 'em to line up an' salute.

Forgettin' her dress for a moment, I turned to Nina an' said, "Quick, get down to Saveway an' commandeer their take-a-number machine."

She nodded an' took off.

The park across from the town hall was startin' to fill up with chickens; stranded motorists an' their passengers; Congregational parishioners; an' people pourin' outta the Baptist church across the square. I spotted the Truck brothers an' several other volunteer firemen about the time they spotted me. We all come together in the middle of the park.

"D.W.," I said. "You think you can round me up a livestock truck?"

He said, "I'll see what I can do."

Patrick Truck tossed Dwayne his keys, sayin', "Take my Jeep, D.W., so you can go 'round traffic."

Dwayne took the keys an' took off. I told Patrick, Richard an' the others to see if anyone was hurt.

Just about then, Nina come back with the number dispenser. People was shoutin' an' carryin' on, so I could hardly think straight. I needed to get their attention, so I took out my pistol an' fired two rounds into the parkway. That did it. There was a short pause in the action. I got on the loudspeaker an' told everyone to take a number an' I'd write up their accidents in order. I finished with, "Line-cutters will be sent to the end of the line."

Meanwhile, the chickens was spreadin' out all over downtown.

a Chinese fire drill

"How many chickens was there?"

The chicken truck driver, a man in his twenties, looked to have aged thirty years in the last half hour. He swallowed an' said, "Five hundred."

The mayor said, "Holy shit!" His Sunday suit was dotted with white specks of feathers.

"No," I told him. "Chicken shit. Everywhere."

Our mayor's a short man with thinnin' gray hair an' a beaky nose, generally good-hearted, but political to the bone. He'd appeared, suddenly, while I was writin' up the truck driver, to ask me where I got off pushin' everybody around. It seemed his car was one of the first to be involved, an' he didn't want to take his turn for service.

"And what makes you think you can discharge a gun on Sunday?" he axed.

I didn't have time to play games. "Get in line, your honor, or you could be the last one I get to."

"Who died and left you king?"

"Well, last time I checked, I was charged with traffic enforcement an' maintainin' the peace."

"You were. You're fired."

"Fine with me." I held out my bullhorn an' clipboard. "Have fun."

The mayor took a step back an' said, "Get back to work.

We'll discuss this later." He stomped toward Nina an' her number dispenser.

I had to grin, 'cause she jerked it away from him an' pointed to the end of the ever-lengthenin' line.

At that point, Rye showed up. I give him my deputy's badge an' said, "By the power vested in me as actin' sheriff of Boone County, I hereby deputize you. Get yourself a safety vest an' get out to County C an' *di*vert some of this traffic."

"Ten-four," Rye said an' took off the way he'd come.

One of the volunteer firemen came back to say they'd found four casualties. Three was minor, the fourth had a possible concussion. All of 'em were on their way to the hospital. He give me descriptions an' license numbers of their vehicles so I could keep my records straight. I sent him off to the other side of town from Rye to direct traffic.

Nina's line thinned out, an' she drifted over to where I was still writin' up the chicken truck driver. In that dress, she was incredibly distractin', so I deputized her, give her a fistful of accident report forms, an' the instruction: "Don't get too creative."

It was a warm mornin' an' looked to be a long one, so I broke off from my writin' to arm-twist the Baptist an' Congregational ministers into vyin' for title of best Good Samaritan. In no time, they had housewives in their Sunday finest hurryin' home to make iced tea an' lemonade, an' Sunday-suited husbands cookin' up a barbecue. I finished writin' up the truck driver an' told him to start roundin' up his stock.

Dwayne showed up with a borrowed stock van that looked like he'd drove it off-road across the state. I had him leave it by the Civil War statue in the park, an' gave him a stack of report forms. "You're deputized," I told him. "Find out what number Nina's workin' off of, an' take the next customer in line."

We made slow progress. By the time we'd gotten sixteen vehicles wrote up, the volunteer firemen'd got back from their hospital run an' had dispatched all the injured chickens. They'd also plucked an' cleaned 'em, an' were commencin' to make lunch.

The flood of "foreign" cars through town slowed to a trickle, which changed to a trickle of local folks as word got 'round that somethin' was doin' in town. Rye meandered in with the last of 'em an' gave me back my badge an' traffic safety vest.

"How'd you get us outta the detour business?" I axed.

"I jus' blocked the road an' put up a sign pointin' the detour back to the highway. People don't seem to care much where they're goin' long as they keep movin'."

"You got that right. Good work."

"Thanks. Now, if you don't mind, I got some business to conduct."

"If you're gonna sell your stuff on Sunday, you gotta pay the Sunday tax."

"Sunday tax? What kind of flimflam is that? If you want a cut, jus' say so. Don't gimme no *Sunday tax.*"

"I ain't foolin', Rye. You wanna sell your stuff here today, you gotta supply paper goods an' plastic forks for this picnic."

"Whyn't you jus' say that?"

"I just did. An' I don't want Burt or the Reverend Elroy on my neck, so keep a low profile with your merchandisin'."

"Teach your grandmother to suck eggs!"

Rye stalked off, an' I took stock again. The Chinese fire drill was beginnin' to look more like a down-home Fourth of July picnic. The chicken truck driver had managed to get a dozen or so hens in the stock truck, though it looked like corrallin' the other 450 might do him in. The park was still full of people an' loose chickens, but the chickens was scratchin' an' the folks was standin' 'round socializin'. Father Ernie'd showed up with more volunteers, includin' Ben an' Martha Rooney, an' refreshments. The Reverend Elroy'd sent a crew to bring tables from the church basement, an' the ladies from all three congregations was loadin' 'em with food. The whole show reminded me of the poster Father Ernie keeps in *his* church vestibule: *If life gives you lemons, make lemonade.*

The last driver I had to write a report for, even though his car was the first to be flattened by the semi, was last 'cause he didn't understand about the number thing. He was waitin', with his wife an' kid, like they had the whole afternoon. I axed him his name, an' he looked around to see who was I talkin' to. The second time I axed, he handed me his wallet an' said, *"No hablo ingles."*

I understand enough Spanish to get that. I looked at his wife—eight months' pregnant, if she was a day—an' said, "Do *any* of you understand English?" All I got was a blank stare.

I yelled for Nina to find me the Spanish teacher.

She said, "Sure, Homer." She was bein' unusually cooperative, but I didn't have time to wonder why.

While we waited for the teacher, I thumbed through the wallet. There was some Mexican money an' a couple of things in Spanish, one looked like a driver's license with his pi'ture. Apart from the fact his name was Lopez, I couldn't understand a word.

The Spanish teacher eventually showed an' jabbered with Lopez for a while, then told me, "This gentleman's name is Haysoos."

I showed her the license. "It says here, his name is Jesus Lopez."

"That's English. In Spanish it's pronounced *HAYSOOS*.

They were on their way from Texas to Chicago to visit relatives when they got turned around, and ended up on the Pennsylvania turnpike—two days ago. They used the last of their money this morning, to fill up their tank."

An' I thought I was havin' a bad week.

I finished fillin' out the report an' gave Mr. Lopez back his wallet. Then I axed the teacher to tell the family to enjoy the picnic. It was the least we could do to make up for their inconvenience. The four of 'em wandered off together.

The chicken truck'd turned over on four cars, two of 'em local folks', but the others belonged to outta-towners; fourteen other vehicles got caught in the chain reaction. The two West Wheeling fellas who do odd jobs for a livin' an' act as an unofficial taxi service for the town were in hog heaven shuttlin' the stranded out to Motel Six. Dwayne resigned as deputy to handle the overflow towin' business from the Shell station, an' the two younger Truck brothers got in some overtime doin' emergency repairs. Still, five of the drivers involved found theirselves with no wheels an' no rooms. When the local ministers got done exhortin' their flocks to take in the strangers, everyone got parceled out but the Lopez family. As they were foreigners, they ended up bein' without a chair when the music stopped.

I felt for 'em. Their car was totaled, an' their paperwork highly suspicious. But short of lettin' 'em camp in the park, or callin' immigration—which would've made me feel as bad as turnin' Rye over to the ATF—I couldn't see what to do. It was time to ax for advice.

I found the Rooneys near the barbecue. When I explained the Lopez deal to Martha, she axed to meet the family. I went to get some food—chicken an' tater salad, greens an' cornbread, chocolate cake an' the best iced tea this side of Atlanta. After I finished, I located the Mexicans.

They was trailin' after the Spanish teacher like ducklings followin' their mother. I explained to her that Martha wanted to meet 'em, an' she made a beeline for the Rooneys with her charges trailin'. After she made introductions—Mrs. Lopez was Maria an' the kid was Jose—an' a brief speech in Spanish to Lopez, he took off his hat an' she skedaddled.

Martha held her hand out; Lopez shook it. Maria looked from Ben to Martha an' smiled shyly. I knew they were all gonna hit it off when the kid trotted over to Ben, patted his knee, an' said, *"Abuelo!"*

"They seem like real nice people," Martha said.

"Yeah. I'd take 'em home with me if I was on my own."

She knew what I meant. I live in my ma's house, the same one I grew up in, with my sister Penny an' her husband an' eight kids. I share a bunk bed with two nephews—they got the top. The oldest boy sleeps on the couch.

Martha said, "Don't worry about them, Homer. They can come home with Ben and me." She looked at Ben. Jose was huggin' the sheriff's leg an' the old man was as near to grinnin' as I'd seen him since his stroke. Martha added, "He misses havin' grandchildren."

After a while, Rye come hurryin' up. He seemed to have gotten over his mad at me. "Homer," he said, "we got a problem." He wouldn't tell me what, made me come see for myself. He pointed at a van that had broke open in the pile up.

I leafed through the report forms on my clipboard 'til I found the paperwork. The driver was a Ken Worth, suspected of havin' a concussion, "found semiconscious and incoherent, transported to the hospital for observation." The van was empty.

There was tracks leadin' away from the back of it that looked like the ones Nina's cat makes, only these was big as dinner plates.

tiger by the tail

The tiger's name was Genius. We found that out by makin' a quick call to the hospital on Rye's cell phone. They put Mr. Worth on, an' he begged me, over an' over, to find his cat. An' keep him safe. An' he said the cat's name was Genius. I had to ask what kind of cat it was—he didn't volunteer. It was a white Bengal tiger, full-growed, an' friendly, prob'ly lonesome after three hours on his own, prob'ly scared stiff. Yeah, right.

I tole him I'd do the best I could an' please put the doc back on. The doctor seemed to think Worth was sane enough, but too concussed to be released any time soon.

If he'd been a ordinary tiger, Genius'd a prob'ly faded into the backwoods, blendin' in at least as well as a paint-ball hunter in a camouflage suit. His problem was that he was white—maybe the first time in Boone County history bein' white wasn't a asset. Genius, friendly as he might be, was bound to attract every reporter an' hunter an' gun nut in the state.

When I first got to be deputy, my ma made me read a thing called *Shooting an Elephant*, by a George Orwell. When I give it back to her, I was pretty sore 'cause it was the kind of downer thing I generally avoid.

She'd said, "You know why I had you read that, Homer?"

"I guess you don't want me to get boxed into shootin' no elephants."

"I guess I don't," she'd said.

Which is why, when Rye got the 30-30 out of his truck I said, "Rye, you shoot that tiger, I'm gonna run you in for malicious damage to property—*if* I can't get the DA to go for murder one."

"Aw, Homer."

" 'Fact, if you even mention he's out there, I'm gonna—"

"Homer," Dwayne Truck's voice interrupted.

I turned 'round fast, ready to lay into *anyone* with somethin' else for me to deal with. *"What?"*

Dwayne looked a little hurt at my tone. "Nina axed me to tell you there's a 'large animal' in her post office. She wants you to come get rid of it."

"We got a small crisis goin' on here, Dwayne. Tell Nina to call a exterminator."

He shrugged an' went off, an' I turned back to Rye. "Where was I?"

"You was just about to put your foot in your mouth one time too many."

"You wanna trade jobs?"

"No. But I ain't gonna track down no tiger for you without my gun."

"That's fair enough. But you don't have to shoot it 'less it comes after you."

We started plannin' our tiger hunt—who we could trust not to panic an' shoot it without reason, how we could catch it alive without elephants, nets, or tranquilizer guns. We were speculatin' on how far it might'a gone an' where it might be now, when D.W. come back.

"Homer, Miz Ross said to tell you the animal in the post office is a live tiger, an' she's gonna send a exterminator after you if you don't come right away."

That took care of one problem.

'Course, it left us with another. The post office is right across the street from the park, where half the population of West Wheeling an' a fair number of friendly strangers were recreatin'. An' I noticed one of the revelers was our local reporter. We didn't need him findin' out there was a tiger in town an' traipsin' across the street to peer in the windows at it, maybe poundin' on the glass to make it look.

I hurried over to the post office, where Nina was sittin' on the porch, tryin'—unsuccessfully—to look relaxed. I sauntered up the steps an' sort of nonchalantly looked in the window. There was a tiger in there, all right—big as a Holstein bull. It was sniffin' 'round in there just like a overgrown house cat. I turned 'round an' swore all present—Nina, Rye an' Dwayne—to secrecy an' said, "I'm open to suggestions."

"I think we oughtta feed him, Homer," Nina said. "When they're well fed, cats use-ly jus' sleep all day. Then maybe we could get one of them state game wardens to come out with a tranquilizer gun an' put 'im to sleep til we get 'im caged."

I said, "Sounds like a plan to me."

An' it prob'ly would'a worked if we could'a got hold of a game warden. As it was, we threw a couple steaks into the post office an' the tiger inhaled them like a chocoholic snarfin' up Whitman's candies. I sent Rye to the Saveway for more meat, an' we all waited to see what the tiger'd do next. He got up to put his paws on the window sill an' look out. In fact, he leaned forward 'til he bumped his nose on the glass. He even batted at it a few times with his big paws.

"Homer," Nina said. "That cat must weigh three hundred pounds. What's to stop him just jumpin' through the glass?"

"He don't know he can do that. Long as he don't *know* he can do it, he won't."

"What if he jus' sees somethin' out here he wants an' goes for it?"

It was a good question. "I guess we'll just have to clear the street so there's nothin' out here for him to see that he might want."

"An' in the meantime," she said, "we'll have to think of a way to get him to go in the back room, where there's bars on the window, so we can keep him in."

Rye got back from the Saveway in time to hear her say that. "Yeah? Who's gonna go in an' close the door on 'im?"

"You get him to go in the back," I said, "I'll go in the front way an' close the door."

The way things was goin', bein' et by a tiger was startin' to look preferable to bein' actin' sheriff in a county with two unsolved murders, three disappearances, an' a three-ring, chicken-pluckin' circus in the center of town.

order restored

It went down pretty much like we planned. Rye an' Nina went 'round back with the rest of the meat. We made Nina the lookout an' gave her a handheld radio. She watched through the barred, back-room window while Rye unlocked the back door. Naturally, the noise attracted the cat's attention an' he come runnin'.

Nina give me the word, an' I slipped in the front, scooted 'round the counter, an' grabbed the back-room door handle.

"Homer!" she yelled. "He's comin' your way."

I froze.

"Homer, he's turned around. He's goin' for Rye!"

Fortunately for all concerned, both doors to the back room open in. When the tiger jumped at Rye, he knocked the back door shut. Then I jerked the front door shut, an' we had the cat bagged.

That was one critter down an' four hundred to go.

Rye got us a Mason jar of brew an' the four of us sat on the porch while we considered the problem.

Across the street, the park was full of people—young families an' old folks; courtin'-age members of both sexes; newlyweds an' old married folks; children of every description; an' chickens—four hundred of 'em. Chickens on the grass an' in the bushes, chickens under the tables an' the cars an' trucks parked along the street. Even a chicken atop the head of the

Civil War statue. The chicken truck driver had given up an' was sittin' on the front bumper of the stock van, swiggin' somethin' out of a paper bag.

Rye said, " 'Cept for them chickens, this'd be a near perfect day." Great minds think alike.

Nina said, "How 'bout we get someone with a cow dog to come an' herd 'em in the truck?"

"Nah," D.W. said. "Most folks spend too much time tryin' to teach their dogs not to chase chickens to go for that."

" 'Sides," Rye added. "You can't *herd* chickens."

All three of 'em looked at me. Nina said, "You're allus jus' full a great ideas, Homer. What do we do?"

I looked across the street an' thought hard. My ma always said, "Live horse an' you'll get grass." I'd a been happy to get even a half-assed idea, just then. An' just then, I did.

A couple middle school–age kids give it to me. 4H-ers. One of 'em, in his Sunday-best suit, grabbed a hen an' yelled to a buddy, "Bet I can get more of 'em than you!"

His friend naturally pounced on the next nearest bird. Both of 'em suddenly found theirselves with the problem of what to do with the bird he had, to free his hands up for another catch.

I stood up an' yelled, "Hey kids!" Both of 'em froze as I started cross the street, trailin' my posse. When I got near enough I didn't have to yell, I pointed at the stock van an' said, "Bring them hens over there. That fella'll give you a nickel for every one you bring 'im live."

The chicken truck driver heard me an' stood up. "In a pig's eye!"

I fixed him with my sternest Law Enforcement frown an' said, "We got fines for litterin' an' creatin' public nuisances, if you get my drift. An', given time, I could prob'ly find half a dozen other laws apply. It'd sure cost you more'n a measly twenty bucks."

He swallowed hard. "I guess a nickel apiece isn't too bad. But what about those . . ." He pointed to the chicken on the barbecue.

"Salvage," I said. "None of the ones we cooked up was alive."

"Are you going to pay me for them?"

I tried to look hurt. "They're your contribution to this party. After all, you convened it." I eyed the bag he'd been pullin' on an' said, "An' it 'pears to me, you're enjoyin' yourself as well as the next man." Which pretty much put an end to his objections.

It took about a minute an' a half for word to get 'round to all the kids about the "easy" money to be made. Then Rye, D.W., Nina, an' I just had to sit there an' keep tally as the young-uns rounded up the stock. Turned out to be the most entertainin' picnic game we'd ever come up with in West Wheeling.

two favors

Rosy-fingered dawn was stealin' the cover of night when my pager went off—right by my ear. I have folks page me at night, so they won't wake my nephews in the top bunk.

I staggered out to the kitchen an' dialed the number that come up. A hoarse voice answered on the first ring. "Yeah."

"Deters. You paged me."

"Homer!" It was Rye. "Homer, I need a favor."

"You got any idea what time it is?"

"Yeah. An' I'm stranded in Okra. Can you come git me?"

I smothered a yawn an' stifled the urge to hang up. "I s'pose. Where in Okra?"

" 'Cross from Calamity Jane's." That explained a lot.

"I'll be along."

Rye looked like he'd been rode hard an' put away wet. He got in the truck an' said, "Thanks, Homer."

I just nodded. I turned 'round an' headed for the Truck Stop. I needed caffeine as much as Rye looked like he did. I said, "Where's your wheels?"

"Must be at Diamond Jim's. Least, that's the last time I 'member seein' 'em." He shook his head. "I got drunker'n Couder Brown last night—woke up in a strange house, in bed with a woman ugly as homemade soap. Must'a been wearin' my beer goggles when we hooked up."

I couldn't disagree.

"I'm gettin' too old for this, Homer. I gotta get serious 'bout findin' a wife or talkin' Nina—"

"Nina's spoke for."

Rye made a face like he'd been gut shot, an' put his hands to his head an' shook it slowly.

"Well," I said, reasonably. "I saw her first."

We ordered breakfast an' didn't talk until it was half gone. Then I axed Rye to go over the disappearance of Roger Devon again.

"Lord, Homer, can't you think a nothin' else?"

"Devon's still missin'."

After we'd mainlined enough coffee to bring Lazarus back, I dropped Rye off by his truck an' swung 'round to the Motel Six. John Peter weren't no happier to see me'n he'd been the last time, but nobody said bein' deputy sheriff was a popularity contest. He wasn't a serious suspect in any of the recent happenin's, so I drove him back to the Truck Stop an' let him get food an' coffee in him 'fore I started grillin' him. He tole me, since his mission an' his clients wasn't confidential, he didn't mind comparin' notes. This last was wishful thinkin' on his part, but I let him wish. He tole me he'd showed Devon's pi'ture 'round, too—with no luck. He'd talked to the Greyhound driver an' various semi drivers that had regular business in the area. If he knew about Angie Boone, he didn't say.

For my part, I tole him what I knew 'bout Puzzle Man—basically nothin'. The other body'd been about twice Devon's age, which ruled Headless out as a candidate for the missin' missionary.

"So unless Roger was abducted by aliens," Peter said, "I think we can assume the swamp victim was he."

"Sheriff Rooney allus tole me when you *assume* you make a *ass* out of *u* an' *me*. So I ain't *assumin'* nothin'."

I could see my wafflin' was gettin' to him. Or maybe it was the limited amenities West Wheeling had to offer sophisticated city folk. "I've been asking about Ash Jackson," he said. "According to everyone, he's bad news."

" 'Spect you ain't talked to his mother."

Peter ignored that. "Even *you* have to wonder about the coincidence of them disappearing at the same time."

"Could be a coincidence, but Ash's gone missin' before. If he'd had a conscience, you might think his conscience was gettin' to him. But since he don't, you could figger he's makin' hisself scarce 'til the heat's off."

"Well, if these bones are all that's left of Roger, a DNA test should prove it. I'm ready to call it quits and, frankly, staying on would just be taking the Devons's money."

"They kin afford it, can't they?"

"That's not the point."

"Do me a favor. Give me another forty-eight hours to clear this up. Maybe I kin give you somethin' firm to tell 'em, even if it ain't real happy news." I was thinkin' of Angie Boone's kid. I couldn't bring back the Devons's son, but mebbe I could put 'em on to a grandchild. I'd have to talk to Angie.

"There's something you're not telling me."

"Call it more of a hunch. I gotta hunch this case is gonna break soon."

"I'll give you forty-eight hours."

Mrs. Ruthless

Mrs. "Ruthless" Groggins is such a plain woman, she'll probably disappear if she ever turns pale. Which is likely why Ruthless married her. No matter how slovenly or hungover he is, he has to look good standin' by her side.

"Rufus ain't here, Sheriff," she tole me.

"Yes, ma'am. Kin you tell me where he might be?"

"Workin'."

That was a novelty. But I didn't say so. I said, "Well, mebbe *you* kin help me."

She waited, not givin' the slightest sign of resentment or curiosity, or even that she'd heard.

"I wonder, could you tell me where Rufus was the night of the seventh, last month? Did he go out, do you recall?"

She stared like she hadn't heard me, for long enough to make me wonder. Then she blinked once an' said, "He was at the rally."

It took me twenty minutes like that to get it out of her that Ruthless'd been away that whole week. An' that *she* hadn't believed he was where he said, either, 'til he'd showed her the newspaper pi'ture. When I axed, "Could I see it?" she'd said, "Sure, Sheriff," an' trotted it out.

The pi'ture showed Ruthless bein' stuffed into a squad car by a black an' white cop team. He was wearin' those wimpy, plastic handcuffs. Under the pi'ture, it said, "A KKK member is arrested by police." I ain't sure I'd want nobody to see me in a situation like that, but then, I ain't Ruthless. Nor desperate, neither.

I noted the particulars in case I needed a reprint, an' I thanked Mrs. Ruthless.

Nina ain't always right.

Angie disappears

When I got to the kitchen, Grandpa Ross actually stood up. He was breathin' 'specially heavy, like he always does when he's excited. He said, "That was fast."

"What was?"

"Can't be five minutes ago I called."

"Maybe you'd best start over. Who was it you called an' what about?"

"You. Well, I talked to Martha Rooney. She said she'd get hold a you."

"About?"

"That dad-blamed girl Nina's had stayin' here stole my gun!"

I looked at the corner where Grandpa kept his twenty-gauge; it weren't there. I said, "Angie?"

"Damn straight!"

"When'd it happen?"

"Not a quarter-hour ago. Nina went off to work. I went in there . . ." He hitched his thumb in the direction of the indoor outhouse. "When I come out the girl was gone an' my gun with 'er."

"Anythin' unusual happen this mornin'? Anybody stop in or call?"

"Might'a been a call—don't know. I never answer the damn thing."

"Anythin' else missin'? Shells or food or money?"

Grandpa huffed an' puffed over to the drawer where he kept his spare shells an' hauled it open. "Shells," he wheezed. He patted his back pocket an' nodded like he was reassured. "You'll have to ask Nina 'bout money. She ain't took nothin' else a mine."

the last straw

One more missin' person was the last straw. I broke every speed record set in Boone County gettin' back to my office, an' by the time I pulled up in front of the town hall, I'd called Martha to have her check with the Boones an' her good old girl network for the missin' girl. Nina was the only one in the post office when I stomped in.

"Where's Angie?"

"Well, good mornin' to you, too, Homer."

"Angie."

"I left her home today, bein' as how our back room is still occupied so she cain't lie down or use the facilities. Tole her I'd give her two dollars a hour to keep a eye on Grandpa."

"That the truth?"

Nina looked insulted an' disgusted. "I ain't even gonna dignify that with—What's wrong?"

"She run off an' took Grandpa's twenty-gauge with her."

"Oh, shit!"

"My words exactly. Where would she'a gone?"

"Back home?"

"I checked. They said no."

"Well." Nina frowned. "How far could she git with no wheels?"

"She prob'ly hitchhiked."

"With a twenty-gauge?"

"You're right. She prob'ly just hijacked a ride."

"This ain't no time for jokin', Homer."

"Who said I was?"

Then Nina changed the subject suddenly. "When's that fella gonna get his cat outta my back room?"

"Doc said they'd let him out tomorrow."

"Good, 'cause that room's gettin' pretty ripe." She must've noticed I was gettin' a bit put out, 'cause she added, "Don't worry, Homer. She'll turn up."

I went back to the office an' called Martha back, after which I called the reverends Elroy an' Burton, Father Ernie, Lucy at Motel Six, Merlin at Best Buy, Charity Nonesuch at the Truck Stop, an' the manager at Saveway. Nobody'd seen Angie Boone. Naturally I called the state cops next, to put out a All Points Bulletin. I gave the dispatcher a description an' said, "She's wanted for grand larceny an' she's armed. Might even be dangerous."

"You been having quite a few missing persons down there in Boone County, wouldn't you say, Deputy? What do you attribute that to?"

"Alien abductions. Sergeant Underhill around?"

"Sure thing."

Dan was chucklin' when he come on the line, so I guessed the dispatcher must've shared my alien theory with him. "Deputy Deters," Underhill said, "I was just fixin' to call you 'bout that last set of prints. I got some good news and some bad news."

"I'm all ears."

"The good news is, one of that last set of prints you sent in matches one we found in the Escort you pulled outta the ravine. Bad news—none of the prints you came up with so far is on file anywhere. But when you find a suspect, you got a good start on makin' a case."

"What about the finger I sent? You get a match on that?"

"I was wonderin' when you'd get around to askin'."

"I ain't s'posed to have to ask. You're s'posed to call an' *tell* me if you found somethin' out."

"Well, ATF asked me to keep it quiet."

"Whose side are you on?"

"You got a point. Seems your victim was an ATF agent—one George Arnold."

"Well, what do you know?"

"Sounds like you knew him."

"Only his ghost, mebbe. He's one of the persons I been missin' of late."

"You think all these missin' persons are connected?"

"You think the Pope's Catholic?"

"When you get it all doped out, let me know. It has the beginnings of a heck of a tale."

Ash Jackson's truck

"Homer," Rye said, over the phone, "I think we found the truck."

I didn't have to ask which one. Ash Jackson's was the only truck missin' I knew of. "Where?"

"Half a mile short of the Truck Stop."

"Don't touch nothin'. I'll be along directly."

The truck was sure enough where Rye said, nosed into the bushes far as it would go off the road. Rye was circlin' it like a kid checkin' out the presents Christmas mornin'. He could scarcely wait for me to git outta my car.

The reason it was ditched was obvious—two flat tires. Even apart from the tires, the truck was pitiful. Ash'd always kept it clean, inside an' out, but it was full of mud an' fast-food wrappers. On the outside, it looked like one of those off-road yahoos had used it to plow a field. You could hardly see the color for the mud.

So we took pi'tures an' dusted it fer prints. I put on latex gloves an' went through the glove box an' under the seat; I found the keys. The only thing remotely interestin' was a few fingerprints on a box of Trojans. I put the Trojans in a evidence envelope, an' called Dwayne to come haul away the truck.

ATF turns up agin

Walkin' into my office was like déjà vu—times three. Three men in suits, one of 'em sittin' at my desk, all with shades an' attitudes. I said, "I 'spect you got your reasons for bargin' in here like you own the place."

The one in my chair showed me his federal ID an' said, "ATF." He was wearin' a gray suit an' flat-heel shoes.

I said, "Yeah. So?"

"We want your file on that John Doe homicide you reported."

"You mean ATF agent George Arnold?"

That set 'em down a peg.

"What do you know about it?" the one in the brown suit axed.

"I know someone killed him an' dumped his remains in a ditch."

"Effing state cops," Brown Suit said.

The third man had on a blue suit, I guess so civilians could tell 'em apart. Brown Suit grabbed the front of my uniform—just like a bad guy in the movies—an' said, "We don't have time for games."

I stared at his hand 'til he let go. "Who writes your dialogue?"

He looked ready to punch me out, but Gray Suit told him, "That's enough." To me, he said, "We would appreciate your cooperation." It looked like his jaw hurt to say it.

"Well, when you put it like that, what kin I do for you?" I pretended I wasn't the only one standin'—in my own office.

"We really need to see your file on the case."

I shrugged. I noticed the cat whisker I'd closed in the file cabinet drawer was missin'. They wouldn't'a axed for the file if they'd been able to locate it. I fished it out of my OUT tray, where I'd left it earlier, an' dropped it on the desk in front of Gray Suit. He skimmed it an' glanced at all the pi'tures. "What'd you do with the negatives?"

"I forget."

He stuffed the file back together an' stood up. "Well, when you remember, put 'em in a safe place. We'll be back."

I was glad I'd thought to make copies of the file. I said, "Don't forget to bring a court order." I waited 'til he was clear of the desk, then sat down an' put my feet on it. When the first one was out the door, I said, "Bye the bye, there was a fella in here last week callin' hisself Arnold."

That got 'em. They stopped an' turned 'round together, like a small flock of pigeons. Gray Suit said, "What did you say?"

I repeated myself.

"What did he look like?"

"Kinda like you. Male Caucasian, six-two, two-hundred pounds, mid-forties. *He* had on snakeskin boots, though."

The three of 'em looked at one another. "What did he want?" Gray Suit axed.

"Said he was lookin' for Ash Jackson."

"Why?"

"Didn't say. Told me to mind my own business."

"Where do we find this Jackson?"

"Can't say. Ain't seen him lately. 'Course with so many

folks out lookin' for him, it's no wonder he's made hisself scarce."

"What would you guess this impostor wanted with him?"

"I dunno. Maybe Ash owed him money."

the state cops lose their car

I might'a made some headway in some of my cases if more didn't keep poppin' up all over. I'd no sooner got rid of the three ATF stooges than the state police dispatcher got on the air to announce a mutual aid call. I was s'posed to come to *their* aid for a change, to the Seven-Eleven at County C an' the highway.

When I got there, Dan Underhill come huffin' outta the store an' slid into the passenger's seat.

"What's up?" I said.

"Grand theft, auto."

"Whose?"

He got real red, an' I suddenly got the pi'ture. "Let me see if this is how it went?" I said. "You stopped here for coffee . . ."

He didn't say yes or no, but I took it for "yes" that he got redder.

"You left your car runnin' an' unattended—just for a second—while you went inside . . ." I glanced at him.

He was lookin' straight ahead, an' I thought he just might break his jaw, it was clenched so tight.

"When you come out, it was gone."

He muttered, "Smart-ass."

"How long ago was that?"

"Twenty minutes."

"Golly, Mr. Dillon, you ain't even broadcast a *de*scription of the car yet! He's prob'ly outta state by now."

"The SOB's got a radio. Anything broadcast'll tell him just what we're doing."

"That's true, Kemosabe, but it'll tell all the good guys, too."

He reached for my radio, but I beat him to it. "Allow me." I described the missin' vehicle in *po*lice lingo—never said it was a *po*lice car, just unit number so-an'-so. Then I axed was the bear-in-the-air hibernatin' today?

"No," he said. "It's up there."

"Good. Hang tight a sec." I took my keys outta the ignition an' got outta the car. He was gonna follow, but I told him to wait. "Lemme see if the clerk gives me the same story you got."

The clerk was a well-padded young thing with Coke bottle–glasses, studyin' the latest portable soap opera like her grade in life depended on it. When she looked up, I give her my brightest smile an' said, "Mornin', darlin'."

Her eyes got big as saucers.

"I'm lookin' into a major crime was just committed, an' I wonder if you could give me some assistance?"

It took her a minute to work all that out, an' she seemed like she was goin' into shock. Finally, she said, "Anything, Sheriff."

"You seen anyone hangin' 'round here while the state trooper was in?"

"The one that lost his car?"

"That one."

She made a face told me Underhill hadn't been diplomatic. "No. He already axed me that."

“Anybody been in here tryin’ to bum a ride today?”

“Just a kid. He left before the trooper came.”

“You tell the trooper about him?”

“No. He didn’t ask.”

“What’d this kid look like?”

“Looked like one of the Jackson clan.”

“I’d be obliged for what else you kin tell me.”

“He wasn’t buying nothing, just hanging around. Looked like he was fixing to steal something soon’s I turned my back. So I threw ’im out.”

I give her another smile an’ said, “You don’t know how much you helped. I certainly am obliged.” When I tipped my hat, I thought she’d swoon. I decided it’d be safer to make my phone calls somewheres else.

hot pursuit

I'd fergot my cell phone, so I got back in my car an' drove to the next pay phone down the road, at a fillin' station. It was one of those convenience phones you don't have to get outta your car to use. I wasn't keen on leavin' my car runnin' with the keys in, an' givin' Dan Underhill the chance to leave *me* on foot. My first call was to the mission school, to confirm Skip Jackson was missin'. He was. The Reverend Mr. Moody tole me in no uncertain terms that I could keep him if I found him, though near as I could tell, his worst infraction had been "setting a horrible example for the other boys."

The state helicopter, meanwhile, was crisscrossin' the area. So my second call was to the state police dispatcher. I explained that, since the car thief had a radio, the best way to get him was to feed him misinformation 'bout the pursuit. "Tell the 'bear' to stay with him, whatever we say we're up to, an' we'll be able to trap him without our radios."

I could tell by his sly grin, Underhill was with me, even before he said, "You *all right,* Vergil."

Boone County's got just two kinds of car thieves. Some steal to get a car or for the money they can make sellin' it. That sort mostly heads for the local "midnight auto parts" to unload their booty or get a quick-change to a horseless carriage of another color. The rest just "borrow" whatever wheels rolls their way an' leave 'em when a better prospect's left unattended.

We checked on the first possibility first. The proprietor's a old geezer, a bit loopy from too many years sniffin' paint fumes. He claimed he hadn't seen our missin' car. He was so quick offerin' to let us tour his place, I guessed he really hadn't. We looked 'round anyway. There was enough suspicious odd parts to justify a search warrant, but none of them looked like it came from a *po*lice car.

When we got back in the cruiser, Underhill said, "He's probably got to the city by now, got it chopped up already."

I said, "I ain't so sure. The clerk said she saw one of the Jacksons hangin' 'round. Tell 'em to swing by Mama J's an' have a look-see."

"A car thief's going to stop on the way out of town to visit his mother?"

I shrugged. "He might if he was only twelve." I didn't tell him about the thoughts I'd entertained at twelve of joyridin' in a cop car. Luckily, none of the then-deputies had been fool enough to leave his keys in.

Just then, the radio come to life, the "bear-in-the-air" reportin' in. "Attention all units. Suspect *ve-hi-cle*'s headin' out on County C. Now he's turnin' south. Yee-haw! We done trapped him! There's no other road out!"

I weren't so sure. I'd never found it, but judgin' from all the times Ash give me the slip when I was tailin' him for speedin', there had to be a back road. I grabbed the radio an' said, "Ten-four. Headin' east on C." Then I turned on my 'mergency lights an' turned west.

Underhill said, "What'n hell are you doin'?"

"Practicin' guile an' deception," I tole him. I turned south on Winesap an' floored it. Usin' the radio, I told the troops, "Deputy Deters, turnin' in Ash Jackson's drive."

"We got 'im now," the helicopter pilot yelled. "Puttin' down on the drive. I got it blocked."

I slowed to turn onto County D as the chopper pilot let out a string of cuss words that'd made Ash Jackson blush. "He lost him," I told Underhill.

The pilot yelled, "Son-of-a-bitch just took off across country—under the trees. I lost him!"

"Do tell," Underwood said. He was eyein' my speedometer—a tad under ninety. I noticed he'd buckled his seat belt. When I reached for the radio, he said, "Let me."

"Next time." I keyed the mike an' started callin' out location reports: "Unit Twenty-eight, ready at County D an' Winesap." "Unit Four, ten-eight at Westerly's drive." "Unit Eighteen, standin' by at County D an' Breech Road." Every time I changed unit numbers, I threw my voice off a little so I sounded like someone else. I was hopin' it would seem to our car thief like a whole posse was blockin' his escape routes.

Underhill grinned, then noticed the speedometer an' went white. Up ahead, I could see the dust cloud raised by somebody drivin' cross-country, comin' up on the roadway. The car itself was outta sight already.

Some *real* state trooper come on the air to announce he had County D blocked east of Goode Swamp.

"Well, get ready," I told him. "This old country-boy car thief ain't stupid enough to go to ground in the swamp. He'll be comin' your way."

Then the chopper pilot reported he had the stolen car in sight, an' no fewer than three other troopers came on to tell him not to "for-God's-sake" lose him again. Things were lookin' up.

But then, Murphy's Law bein' S.O.P., there was screech of brakes, an' the cop that was blockin' County D screamed into his radio, "He's done a one-eighty! He's headin' west again!"

I figgered I had about one minute, given my speed an' his. I grabbed my mike an' yelled into it. "Posse, hold your positions. Keep all them side roads blocked. If he's goin' anywhere, it's gonna be Goode Swamp." Then, 'cause I couldn't 'member all the unit numbers I'd made up, I let out a series of ten-fours in different voices.

We come up onto the railroad overpass just west of Goode Swamp Road, an' I laid a double line of rubber stoppin' the car on top of the bridge. Just east, I could see the stolen squad headin' at us, with a state car hangin' on its rear bumper, an' the "bear" hoverin' overhead. I swung my car 'round, sideways to traffic, an' stopped it square across the bridge, driver's side facin' east. A bicycle couldn't'a squeezed past either end. An' there was no way to go 'round the bridge. I told Underhill he better get out an' take cover.

"Ain't you comin'?" he axed.

"In a minute."

The stolen car kept comin'. It passed Goode Swamp Road doin' seventy—at a guess—an' closed up the distance to the overpass without slowin'. The state trooper behind him lost his nerve an' slowed down. Underhill shouted somethin' I didn't get.

The stolen car came at me up the incline like a trick truck at the fairgrounds fixin' to jump a line of cars. I stayed put an' hit my siren—one short WROR.

Then the car thief braked. The tires screamed an' left heavy exclamation marks on the road. The car stopped three inches short of my door.

Underhill an' three other troopers swarmed 'round the car with guns drawed. The driver threw his hands in the air.

To give the gravity of the situation time to penetrate the

thick skull of the tow-head behind the wheel, I took my time gettin' outta my car. So the state boys had him out an' cuffed by the time I strolled up.

"Gentlemen," I told 'em, "this here's Skip Jackson."

I make a deal

"I ain't talkin' 'til I git a lawyer." Skip folded his arms an' stood with his feet braced like a yearlin' mule. "I got rights."

I had to fight hard to keep from grinnin'. But the boy'd be dangerous as Ash if someone didn't set him straight soon, an' *that* wasn't funny. "Is 'at so?" I said. "You been watchin' too much TV, boy. Bein' a minor, you got only whatever rights I say."

I could see his attitude waver a bit, so I figgered I'd throw him off by changin' tactics. I sat back agin the edge of my desk an' said, "What do you think I oughtta do with you?"

"I dunno."

"Well, what'd you do to someone you caught stealin' your car?"

"Wasn't your car." I gave him a look, an' he said, "Prob'ly kill 'im."

I didn't come back at that, an' after a time, the weight on his conscience did the job for me. He got red, then redder. Finally, he blurted out, "I jus' needed a ride, an' wouldn't nobody pick me up. An' the turkey was jus' beggin' me to take his car—leavin' the keys in . . ."

I nodded; made sense to me. "Why'd you leave the mission?"

"I been hearin' all kinds a rumors 'bout people

disappearin'—Mr. D. an' Angie. An' I heard you found a dead guy—murdered—an' I jus' had'a find out what's goin' on."

I nodded again. "That still leaves us with what to do with you. You're a minor, so it looks like it's gonna be *re*form school."

"I'll be good. Mr. Moody would give me another chance if you axed him."

"Mebbe. But why should I stick my neck out for a car thief?"

"I was jus' borrowin' it. Didn't you ever 'borrow' a car when you were a kid?'

Well, that got me. "I plead the fifth."

He grinned. "I won't do it again if you give me another chance."

"Your word on it?"

"Cross my heart'n hope to—" I fixed him with a look. "My word."

"Okay. We just gotta convince the state *po*lice they oughtta drop the charges."

"You think you can?"

"Mebbe. 'Course, you screw up again, they'll kill both of us."

Two hours later, when he come back for his "prisoner," Sergeant Underhill was still steamed.

"Dan," I told him, "it seems to me leavin' your keys in is contributin' to the delinquency of a minor chile. An' if you prosecute for car theft, it's gonna get all over that you left your car unattended against state law an' department policy. Press'd love to get their hooks on a story like that. An' if they did, County Welfare'd *have* to press charges."

"Whose side are you on, Deputy?"

"I'm a officer of the law. I ain't s'posed to take sides."

"Well, who's gonna tell 'em?"

"I am," Skip piped up.

"Stay outta this, young 'un," I said. "Well, Dan?"

He looked at me like I was a shady car salesman with a lemon to unload. "What'd you have in mind?"

"Skip here's a genuine *phe*nomena—first member of his clan's got a shot at goin' to college. An' bein' as he ain't stupid, I figger he won't blow it by stealin' no more cars."

"What's to guarantee that?"

"What if I agree to be his parole officer?"

Underhill shook his head. "He doesn't need a parole officer. He needs a keeper. The Reverend Mr. Moody said don't bring him back."

"Okay."

"You nuts?"

"I'll try almost anythin' once. You agree to suspend charges, I'll take custody 'til he's eighteen."

"What about Child Welfare?"

"They'll be happy to have someone they can sucker into takin' 'im."

Underhill thought about it for all of thirty seconds. "Done! God help you." He turned to Skip, whose jawed nearly dislocated fallin' open. "Just remember, we're only gonna *suspend* charges. You keep your nose clean or we'll throw the book at you."

Which is how, in the middle of everythin' else, I become a foster dad.

Ransom Thomas

"Homer, I 'membered the name on that missin' Wanted poster." Nina was all out of breath from runnin' up the stairs to my office. She was a little heated, an' glowed. I had to catch *my* breath. "It was Ransom Thomas. I 'membered 'cause he's distant cousin to the Okra Thomases an' a even more distant cousin to Ash Jackson. Ash's ma was in fer some stamps an' happened to mention one of her nieces on the Thomas side was fixin' to tie the knot."

Now that she mentioned it, I did vaguely 'member seein' that name on the poster the day I'd axed Nina to lunch. I'd been preoccupied or I'd'a noticed the face, too. No matter. I could get the particulars faxed to me by the state cops, along with a better pi'ture'n the original. I said, "Much obliged, Nina."

"Much obliged? That's all you got to say?"

"See you later?"

"Humph."

She stalked out, an' I called the state police. A half hour later, my fax machine spit out a piss-poor pi'ture of Thomas. He looked about nineteen an' scared. I wondered what a bank surveillance pi'ture of him robbin' the bank'd look like. Prob'ly make you wonder why he wasn't laughed outta the bank when he announced the stickup. He didn't look like anyone I'd seen lately, but I made a couple copies anyway.

Just to get on Nina's good side, I dropped the first one off at the post office. An' to be on the safe side, I axed about Thomas when I made my rounds.

manhunt

Besides marshalin' the force of numbers, buildin' a posse is a good way to get all the hotheads together where you can keep a eye on 'em. I spent a hour playin' with the state police identi-sketch computer, endin' up with a fair likeness of the Arnold impersonator. Armed with that, an' my pi'ture of Devon, an' a year-old school picture of Angie—enlarged 'til it looked like someone else—I recruited my posse. No one sober was turned away. I even took Ruthless Groggins.

We started at Ash Jackson's place. We searched it through an' through, then searched every shed, abandoned barn, an' unlocked cellar in the town. We found stolen property, a missin' dog, an' a toddler that'd wandered off from his mother. By late afternoon, we positively knew where all of my missin' persons wasn't. An' my posse was all adventured out, ready for a cold one an' a evenin' of TV. We ended up at Diamond Jim's, where I bought a round of beers. Rye was just standin' another round when my pager went off.

The number was familiar—my sister Penny's—an' I answered, though I figured it was likely another hassle. She told me she was takin' Skip home with her for dinner an' she'd see he did his homework after. I told her I had a few things to finish up at the office an' I'd be along. Also, I owed her one. Truth is, I'd forgot all about bein' a new dad.

That left me with nothin' to stop me askin' Nina out to

dinner. I was standin' on the porch with my hat in my hand when she come out to lock up at five. I axed would she do me the honor of breakin' bread with me, an' she was so flabbergasted, she forgot to say no.

When we got back to the post office, I noticed the light on up in my office. Whatever I'd planned for the rest of the evenin', investigatin' a burglary wasn't it, but I was sure I'd locked up 'fore I left. An' the town hall ain't all that secure a facility. So I headed over to see what was up. Even though I told her not to, Nina tagged along.

The back door'd been kicked open. Whisperin' to Nina to at least stay behind me, I took the steps two at a time. Nina stayed right on my heels. So, when I pulled up short, just inside my open office door, she run right into me.

I was beginnin' to feel like someone in a rerun of the movie *Groundhog Day*, like I'd played the scene so many times I was goin' crazy.

Nina said, "Homer, what?—" then "Homer, he's got a gun!"

The man sittin' in my chair, with his feet on my desk—*again,* pointin' his .357 at us said, "With you beatin' the bushes all over town, I had to hole up where nobody'd think to look."

"Well," I said, "you can't stay outta sight with every light on in the place."

"Actually, Deputy, I was keepin' the light on for you. We gotta talk."

a hostage situation

"I thought I heard you was dead," Nina said to him.

"Rumors of my death've been exaggerated."

"Well," I said, "you ain't Lazarus. An' I got it on good authority agent George Arnold—the real one—is dead."

"You're too smart for your own health," the man who wasn't Arnold tole me.

"I been tole that. You want a drink?"

When I stepped over to the filin' cabinet, he shook the .357 an' said, "I want Ash Jackson." He put his feet down an' stood up to help hisself to my gun, which he shoved in his belt, an' the liquor in my filin' cabinet. "Where is he?"

Starin' down the barrel of a gun don't bring out the cooperative in me. I said, "He went out to shit an' the hogs ate him."

Hearin' myself say that made me think—what if it weren't pigs, but bears? Maybe I'd been thinkin' about this whole disappearin' thing backwards. What if it weren't Ash shot Devon, but Devon somehow'd shot Ash? It'd prob'ly be self-defense, but Devon mightn't want to take his chances with our local law, particularly with Ash havin' so many relatives in the county. Devon killin' Ash'd solve a lot of questions in the case without contradictin' anythin' Rye'd tole me 'bout what went down that night. It'd also explain why Angie Boone might be in Ash's truck, in Okra, weeks after Ash an'

Devon disappeared. If Devon'd killed Ash, he'd of had to have help gettin' outta there when he ditched his car to make it look like Ash had killed him. Why not from his special friend Angie, the mebbe mother of his chile? With Ash outta the way, they could've used his truck 'til they run outta gas money. Then they could'a ditched it—someone did. Which left me with a new question: Where were they?

"Earth to Homer!" Nina shoutin' brought me out of my thinkin' spell.

"Yes, ma'am."

"Homer, Mr. ATF agent, here, axed you a question!"

"What's that?"

The phony Arnold sneered. "Can you give me a single reason why I shouldn't put an end to your sorry career as a comedian with a bullet through your skull?" But he was pointin' the gun at my chest.

"Well," I said, tryin' hard to think what he'd do if he suspected what I suspected happened. "If you do that, you'll never find out what happened to Ash."

"Where is he?"

In Hell, I thought. But I wasn't ready to say so just yet. "I believe Nina's got his forwardin' address at the post office."

"An' I s'pose you think I oughtta march the two of you right over there—in the dark—to get it?"

"I plead the fifth."

He cocked the gun he had pointed at me.

"You shoot him, you'll never git the address!" Nina said. " 'Cause I'll know you're jus' gonna shoot me soon's you have it. So I'll never give it to you."

The Arnold impostor thought about that long enough for me to soak through my tee shirt an' Kevlar underwear with sweat. Finally, slowly, he uncocked the gun. But he kept it pointed at my chest. He axed me, "Where's your handcuffs?"

"On the back of my belt."

"Put your hands on top of your head an' lace your fingers together."

I did.

"Now stand real still." He redirected the gun toward Nina. "You, bitch, stay put or I'll kill you."

Nina's jaw clenched an' she shoved it forward but she didn't say yes or no.

Our captor walked 'round the desk 'til he was behind me. I didn't turn round to see exactly where, but I could feel my back hairs risin'. Mr. Not-Arnold took the cuffs outta their holder an' dropped 'em on the desk. He went back where he'd been 'fore an' said, "Put one of them on your right wrist, Deputy." He didn't have to ax was I right-handed. He'd noticed.

I did what I was told.

"Now, bitch," he said to Nina. "You back up 'til you're butt-up-tight against the deputy." When she done that, he sniggered, then said, "Now, Deputy, put your right arm round her waist."

It was one order I didn't much mind takin', an' I think Nina could feel it, cause she blushed redder'n a cherry tomato.

"Now, Deputy," the artificial Arnold said, "put that other handcuff on her *left wrist*."

I could see where he was goin' with this. If you got one set of handcuffs an' two prisoners to transport, makin' 'em walk right on top of each other, or cuffin' 'em so that one's gotta walk backwards in order for 'em to walk side by side, makes great sense. Makes it hard for 'em to run off. I couldn't help myself. I said, "Pretty slick."

He grinned. "Learned that from a little son-of-a-bitch sheriff's deputy in Cook County jail. Some day I'm gonna go back there an' kill 'im." He suddenly noticed Nina's left hand was still free, an' that put a end to his good mood. He recocked the gun an' snarled, "I ain't got all week."

I reached 'round Nina with my left hand an' closed the handcuff on her wrist.

He said, "That's better." He walked 'round behind us an' put the gun to my head.

This time, I could feel Death's cold fingers squeezin' my heart. He noticed my discomfort. He laughed an' tole us, "Put your hands up over your heads." When we did, he squeezed the cuffs tighter 'round our wrists, all the time keepin' the gun to my head. I didn't try nothin'. Besides, Nina was still in his line of fire.

"Now put your hands down in front of you. Hold hands like you's sweet on each other."

That wasn't hard to do, neither. An' if Nina didn't like it, she never let on.

rescue

"He's gonna shoot us, ain't he, Homer?"

"Looks that way."

She sagged agin me a mite. It was the nearest I ever seen to Nina showin' signs of weakenin'. After a bit she whispered, "Ain't no one I'd rather die with, Homer."

"Don't think 'bout that," I whispered back. "I need you to keep your wits sharp." I had another thought an' whispered, "Too bad you ain't got a hairpin—we could use it to get outta this."

"Would a hat pin do?"

"Might."

As Not-Arnold said, "Shut up, you two!" she magicked a hat pin from somewhere in her clothes.

It wasn't easy tryin'a jimmy the ratchet on the handcuff on Nina's wrist an' walk with her pressed up agin me, but by the time we'd got over Cross Street, I'd managed. As the cuff dropped loose, I put my cheek against her head, so my mouth was by her ear an' whispered, "Soon's we're through the door, run for your twelve-gauge."

She didn't say nothin', jus' nodded.

We went up the steps an' stopped at the door. Our jailer said, "You got your key, bitch?"

Nina said, "Yes," sulky like. She was still holdin' the loose cuff in her left hand, while she dug around in her pocket with the other. She pulled out the key an' unlocked the door.

"Get inside," False Arnold said.

We did. The room was dark, an' soon as she was through the doorway, Nina dodged forward an' ducked behind the counter. I stepped aside an' switched on the light.

Nina come up over the counter with the gun cocked an' aimed.

"Arnold" didn't even raise his gun. He stepped into the room an' laughed. There was a gut-flippin' click when Nina pulled the trigger, an' the hammer fell on a empty chamber. Nina froze. Judgin' by the look on her face, she was scared shitless. She hadn't shot him but she'd sure as hell pissed him off.

He pointed his gun at me an' kicked the door shut. "Put your hands out to your sides an' git up against the counter. Quick!"

I done what he said.

"Turn around."

I turned.

"Now, spread your legs."

I spread 'em.

"Put your hands behind your back."

Agin, I followed orders.

He held the muzzle of the gun agin the back of my skull while he snapped the loose cuff on my free wrist. I felt a wave of collywobbles comin' on, but I kept my mouth shut.

He grabbed the back of my collar an' jerked me 'round the end of the counter, keepin' the gun against my head.

"Throw the gun over by the door, bitch," he tole Nina.

She turned white as paper. She tossed the gun where he said.

Tryin' to get his attention off her, I said, "He must'a stole the shells when he took the poster."

Nina's eyes showed her surprise. "Ransom Thomas?"

He chuckled.

"You could'a saved yourself the trouble," I tole him. "That pi'ture was twenty years old. Even I'd'a had trouble recognizin' you."

"I couldn't take the chance, could I?"

He shoved me hard at the wall where the posters was pinned. I hit it with my right shoulder, an' it took fast footwork to keep from goin' down. I turned to face Thomas.

He snarled, "Enough of this horseshit!" an' pointed the gun at my left leg.

There was a loud BANG! The room filled with the smell of smokeless powder. My leg felt like it'd connected with a Louisville slugger in the hands of Joe DiMaggio. 'Fore I could shift my weight, the leg went out from under me. Without my arms free to break the fall, I dropped, smashin' my left shoulder an' the side of my head agin the counter. Thomas followed through with a kick aimed at my teeth. I scooted far enough back—pushin' with my good leg—to save my head, but there was a crack like a twig snappin' when he connected with my collarbone.

At that point, Nina lost it. "Don't kill him!" she screamed.

Thomas cocked the gun an' pointed it at me. "The next one's gonna be higher up an' in the middle."

The pain in my leg didn't distract me none from the queasy feelin' *that* give me.

Nina actually cried. "Please don't! Please don't kill him! I'll do anythin' you want. Please!"

We both stared at her, an' my faith in her ingenuity was restored. She threw *a look* at the door to the back room, then looked at Thomas like she was tryin'a figure whether he'd seen her lookin' at the door. Then she scurried over to her desk. "I'll get you the address. Anythin' you say."

Her plan worked. Findin' out what she didn't want him to see in the back room was suddenly more important to him than havin' Ash's address. He went to the door.

"Please, Mr. Thomas. Don't go in there."

If I didn't know better, *I* would'a been convinced.

Thomas grinned an' said, "What's in there?"

"Just A.B. She ain't involved in this."

"Who's A.B.?"

"Angie Boone. She's been stayin' here since her folks threw her out, sleepin' in the back."

"With all this noise?"

"She's deef."

Thomas laughed an' shifted the gun to his left hand so he could open the door with the other. It was dark inside. He reached in an' flipped the switch next to the door. "Come on out, Angie," he said. Nothin' happened. It was clear he was of two minds. He couldn't check out the back room without takin' his eyes off Nina for a second, an' he'd finally got smart enough to see that was a dumb thing to do.

Still, "Angie" wasn't comin' out. He was shiftin' the gun back to his right hand when two things happened at once: Nina threw the postal regulations at him with all the force she could put behind it. An' Genius let out the most God-awful yowl ever been heard in Boone County.

Between the flyin' book an' the racket, Thomas let go the gun, which went sailin' into the back room. He was about to go in after it when he must'a spotted Genius. He backed out the doorway fast, an' slammed the door. There was a loud thud as Genius hit the other side of it, then a roar like the MGM lion.

Thomas called Nina a "effin' bitch" an' pulled my gun outta his belt.

Nina backed off as far as she could, into the little space behind me, against the wall, 'tween the counter an' the desk.

Neither of them paid me any mind.

Thomas snapped back the hammer an' took a step towards Nina. I shifted on my left side an' hooked my left foot behind his. When he threw his weight forward on the foot, I cocked my right leg back an' put everythin' I had into shovin' my boot heel through his knee. My left foot kept his foot from budgin'. There was a satisfyin' crunch as my boot connected. Then there was a scream, followed by a second crunchin' sound as Nina come down on his gun hand with both her boots.

Thomas passed out.

I managed to keep it together a while longer, even after he landed on top of me. Pretty soon faces started to show over the side of the counter. Nina kneeled next to me, in the blood, an' lifted my head an' shoulders on her lap.

I grinned up at her an' said, " *'Lady, shall I lie in your lap?'* " Nina went from snow white to rose red. " *'I mean, my head upon your lap?'* "

She started yellin' for the paramedics, like my mind was what was hurt. Everybody else seemed to be yellin', too, but I couldn't get about what.

"Nina!" I said. I felt myself goin' down for the count an' had to get somethin' settled 'fore I passed out.

"What is it, Homer?" She was scared pea green.

I took a minute to 'member what, durin' which time she an' everyone else seemed to be holdin' their breath. I nodded at Thomas. "He's under arrest. If he comes to, you read him his rights." I couldn't get out my Miranda card with my hands cuffed behind me. Luckily, Nina figured it out an' found the card. ". . . An' tell Rye . . . to find that city fella . . . Peter. Don't let him leave town."

The last thing I 'member was seein' Skip Jackson starin' down at me in slack-jawed wonder, an' Nina sayin', "Homer, if you die, I'll never speak to you agin."

a heavenly angel

I woke up in heaven. At least, I was surrounded by bright light an' feelin' no pain. An' there was a angel holdin' my hand. I blinked an' noticed she'd been cryin'—her nose an' eyes was all red.

"What's a matter, angel?" I sounded drunk.

"Homer, you're alive!" she said, with Nina's voice.

"Nina?"

"Jus' take it easy, Homer. I'll get the nurse."

Next time I come 'round, I knew I'd been found out an' sent where I belonged. I was burnin' up, dyin' of thirst, an' even my hair hurt. Satan hisself was watchin' for me to open my eyes. I said, "What'd I do to deserve this?"

"Tried to knock down one too many windmills with a broom handle." Rye's voice. He grinned.

I seem to 'member tellin' him, once, about Don Quixote. "What happened?"

"Don't you 'member?"

"Yeah. But I wanna hear your version."

He told me. An' as he did, it all come back to me.

"What day is it?" I axed.

"Thursday."

I'd been out cold two days.

"Nina said you tole Ransom you knew where Ash's hidin'

out," Rye said. "That true?"

"I dunno, mebbe. Nina give you my message about Peter?"

"Yup."

"Well?"

"We got 'im *de*tained at the post office." I waited, an' Rye went on. "When we took you to the hospital, we sprung Mr. Worth an' had him get his tiger outta the back room. Damn thing's tame as a pet dog. Then we hosed out the cat shit an' put Mr. Peter in there for safe-keepin'."

"You read him his rights?"

"Yup. Only we ain't figgered out the charges yet."

"Obstructin' justice, for one. Tell the DA to start with that an' we'll see how cooperative Mr. Peter is 'fore we decide on other things. He must be madder'n a sack full of cats."

"Well, he carried on for a time, but we told him we was makin' a fortune off him—chargin' folks to peep at the crazy man through the back winda. He pretty much clammed up after that."

I tried to nod, but it hurt, so I said, "Do me a favor?"

"If it ain't too outrageous."

"Go out to Ash Jackson's an' have a look 'round. Take Nina an' arrest anybody you find don't belong there."

"Who're you expectin'?"

"A killer, mebbe. So be careful."

"What if we don't find nothin'?"

"Then go over to the Motel Six an' ax Lucy to let you into George Arnold's room—same thing as with Ash's place. If you don't find nobody there, try Peter's room."

"You gonna tell me what this's about?"

I escape

I'd had it with the hospital, but even I ain't crazy enough to try an' drive home with a three-day-old bullet hole in my leg. So after Rye left, I called Martha an' axed her to scare me up one of our two unofficial cabs.

"What for, Homer?" she axed.

"I'm fixin' to blow this pop stand, an' my wheels are at the town hall."

"They can't be releasing you so soon."

"*They* got nothin' to do with it."

I said I'd be ready in a half hour; Martha said she'd see what she could do. Then I rung for the nurse an' axed for my clothes. I got two nurses, who come in empty-handed.

"You can't get up," the first one said. "You've lost a lot of blood."

"That explains why I feel like a quart low."

But that weren't the case, the nurse tole me. "When folks heard you needed blood, Sheriff, they just flocked in to donate. You must be related by blood to half the county now."

That weren't nothin' new.

"Yeah," the second nurse said. "You even got some colored blood in you."

"What color?"

"Why, red of course."

"That's good enough for me." That seemed to confuse her. I turned to the first nurse an' said, "You gonna get my pants, or do I have to walk outta here buck nekked?"

She blushed, an' they scurried off. When the first nurse come back, she was carryin' a set of those blue pajamas doctors wear in the operatin' room. "I'm sorry, Sheriff," she said, an' she really did seem sorry. "The state police took your clothes for evidence. Since you're bound an' determined to get up, you can borrow these."

I thanked her an' told her to clear out an' let me have some privacy. After a bit of back an' forth, she did.

By the time I was dressed, the nurse come back with reinforcements. The doctor repeated what she'd tole me, an' when I tole him I was still leavin', axed me to sign a paper promisin' I wouldn't sue him or the hospital if I died from leavin' against their advice.

Think about that.

They insisted on wheelin' me out the front door in a wheelchair—it give me a new perspective on Ben's state of affairs. Martha was waitin' in the van she drives Ben around in. She had Haysoos with her.

I axed her, "Where's Ben?"

"Maria's watchin' him for a while."

I was feelin' pretty ropey by the time they got me in the van. Martha tole me she was takin' me to her house to convalesce; I was too far gone to argue. I closed my eyes an' tole her to wake me when we got home.

But there's no rest for the wicked. We hadn't got outta the hospital driveway 'fore Rye came on the air to ask Martha to get in touch with me.

I got on the radio. "What is it, Rye?"

"Homer, you're sprung!"

"That's right. What do you need?"

"Nina an' me followed your orders an' we got two prisoners in custody. What do we do next?"

"Bring 'em to Rooney's."

"Sure thing."

"An' Rye, swing by the post office an' fetch that city fella, too."

"Ten-four."

By the time we got to Rooney's I was ready to go back to the hospital. I noticed there was some new outdoor furniture in the yard—half a dozen Adirondack chairs. An' a matchin' chaise newly made outta old cedar boards. I remarked on it, an' Martha told me Haysoos was a carpenter. "He's been earnin' his keep fixin' things an' makin' us these nice chairs."

I axed could I maybe try out the chaise 'til Rye an' Nina got there.

Martha said, "Just make yourself t'home."

early retirement

When I woke up, it seemed like a rerun of Sunday—without the chickens. The yard'd filled with cars an' trucks, an' Martha an' Maria was layin' on a spread that'd do any restaurant proud. Most of the main players from Sunday's comedy was onstage, too—Father Ernie an' the two reverends, Rye an' Nina an' the Truck brothers, Ben an' the Lopez family, an' the mayor. Even Skip an' Grandpa'd turned up.

Martha noticed I was awake an' came bustlin' up with a glass of lemonade. "How're you feelin', Homer?"

I sighed. "I been better. But I guess we'd best get this show over with. Looks like everybody's here but the state *po*lice."

"Oh, they're on their way. Sergeant Underhill called to ask that you not start without him."

At that point, Rye noticed I was conscious an' brought his prisoners over for my inspection. One of 'em was Angie Boone, lookin' teed-off an' surly. The other was a man I'd never met. I said, "Roger Devon, I presume."

He blushed an' nodded.

"What do you got to say for yourself?"

"I think I should talk to a lawyer."

"We seem to be havin' a epidemic of that lately."

Then there was a flash of red an' white light, an' sun gleamin' off chrome. The state law had arrived. Sergeant

Underhill parked his car an' sauntered over. Somebody give him a chair. To me, he said, "Nice uniform."

I let that one go.

Then folks all pulled up chairs or sat around on the grass. Even Mr. Peter folded his arms an' stood within earshot, though he pretended not to be listenin'. When everybody'd got settled, Underhill said, "You can commence."

"This all started," I said, "when Roger Devon come to teach at the mission school, where he met Angie. They got to be good friends. That pissed off Ash Jackson." I looked round an' felt like Jessica Fletcher at four minutes to eight. Everybody was waitin' for my explanation, even Devon an' Angie. Just to build suspense, I thought I'd stall a little. I turned to Devon an' said, "You gonna make a honest woman of her?"

He turned red an' scowled. "We've been married three months."

"Good for you. Well, feel free to jump in any time I misspeak.

"Anyway, Ash took it in his head to eliminate the competition—kinda like that fella in *The Legend of Sleepy Hollow*—he figgered to run Roger off." To Roger, I said, "An' you tole him why that wouldn't work."

Angie jumped in. "We showed him the paper."

"Which made him mad enough to kill."

"He was gonna shoot Roger. He said if I was a widow, I'd be back on the market."

"Why'd you dump him in Goode Swamp?"

"I didn't want to be lynched," Devon said. "He had a lot of relatives."

"I think you underestimate our population," I said.

Devon said, "Angie told me—"

"Young wives are often sure they're right, when they ain't, but it's a moot question.

"So you decided to lay low 'til the heat was off 'cause you weren't leavin' without your wife, an' if you an' Ash an' Angie all disappeared at once, there'd a been a posse raised."

"Yes."

"An' you figgered since Ash didn't need his house no more, you might as well use it."

"I was inside when you came around and left that note."

"Were you there when the house got trashed?"

Devon nodded. "The lunatic kicked the door in and started going through the place like a hurricane. I barely got out before he saw me."

"So you was forced to find somewhere else to stay." I frowned at Mr. Peter.

"Yes," Devon said.

"An' *you* found him hidin' out at the Motel Six," I said to Rye.

"That's right," Rye said. "Along with Angie."

"I guess that accounts for everybody," I said. "Any questions?"

"Where does Ransom Thomas fit in?" Underhill axed.

"Well, they never recovered the money he took in the bank job. My guess is, he left it with Ash. An' when he got out . . ." I left the sentence unfinished.

Folks had started to drift into conversations of their own, when the mayor sidled up to me. "Aren't you gonna arrest him?"

I was gettin' tired. I sighed. "I done already, mayor. ATF's got him."

"I meant Devon—for shootin' Ash."

I had to laugh out loud. "Devon didn't shoot Ash. Devon probably couldn't hit the side of a barn he was leanin' against. *Angie* shot Ash. An' if it wasn't self-defense, it was husband defense, which in my book is justifiable homicide."

The mayor turnt bright red before Martha could bail him out by changin' the subject.

"Mr. Mayor," she said. "Ben an' I have been talkin' it over. An' we've decided to take early retirement. Effective immediately."

Everyone looked at Ben, who gave a lopsided grin an' nodded with the whole upper half of his body.

The mayor was flustered. "But what'll we do for a sheriff 'til the next election?"

"Why, you'll appoint Homer, of course."

"Good choice, mayor," someone said. Someone else whistled.

Which is how I come to be sheriff.

Then I went to sleep.

how it all come out

Nina an' me was settin' on Grandpa Ross's back porch a few weeks later with a quart of Rye's best brew, enjoyin' the full moon an' celebratin' me solvin' my first homicide. Nina was wearin' short, tight cutoffs an' a man's white dress shirt with the tails tied together in front so she looked like Daisy Mae.

Admirin' her legs, I could feel my blood pressure rise—among other things. As far as I could tell—she wasn't noticin' any part of *my* anatomy, much less admirin' it.

"Homer," she said, "you ever been drunk?"

"Why'd you ask?"

"Just occurred to me, I never seen you outta control. Never even heard mention of you bein' drunk. Ever."

"What's the difference?"

"Drunkenness in a man is a great fault."

"Regular drunkenness is a fault, in a man *or* woman. Occasional drunkenness is a natural state. You ever been drunk?"

"I axed you first."

"Once. No, twice. Once in the service."

"What was the other time?"

"When I was eight. My daddy left his jug down where I could get into it. I swear he did it on purpose so I'd get sick an' leave the stuff alone."

"Which is just what happened."

Like I may'a mentioned, Nina's always been sharp.

"Which is what happened. You ever been drunk?" I axed her.

"Nope."

"How's that?"

"Momma always tole me if I got drunk, men'd take advantage. Was she right?"

"Some men would."

"How 'bout you, Homer. If I got drunk, would you take advantage?"

I gave her what I hoped was a sly leer. "Whyn't you get drunk an' let's see?"

She punched me in the upper arm. "*Ho*mer!"

Did I mention she punches like a mule kickin'?

"Hey, that hurt! I oughtta run you in for assaultin' a peace officer."

She moved over closer an' gently touched the spot she'd hit. "I didn't mean to hurt you. Want I should kiss it, an' make it better?"

That sounded promisin'. I looked to see if she was makin' fun of me, but she didn't seem to be sneerin'. I nodded. She kissed my arm, an' that *did* make it better.

"You got any other spots hurt, Homer?"

I 'membered that great scene in *Raiders of the Lost Ark*, where Indiana Jones keeps pointin' to various places on hisself he figures it's okay for Marian to kiss. An' she kisses every one. I figured it was worth a try, but there was somethin' naggin' at me. "Nina, are you drunk?"

"Not yet, Homer."

I wasn't sure I could believe her.

She moved a little closer an' sort of leaned against me an' said, "Meanwhile, you got any other spots?"

I pointed to my gun-shot leg, an' she kissed it. When I

pointed to my shoulder, she kissed that, too. Naturally I pointed to my chin, then a little higher up.

In the end, it *was* pretty much like that scene from *Raiders*. Only *I* didn't fall asleep.

About the Author

Michael Dymmoch is the author of the Jack Caleb/John Thinnes mystery series, and *The Fall*, a novel of romantic suspense. Michael has served as President and Secretary of the Midwest Chapter of Mystery Writers of America, and newsletter editor for the Chicagoland chapter of Sisters in Crime.